THE HOUSE OF THE RED BALCONIES

A.J. DEMAS

The House of the Red Balconies

A.J. Demas

Cover by Flora Kirk

THE HOUSE OF THE RED
BALCONIES

CHAPTER 1

"BY THE GODS, HYLAS," said Governor Loukianos, leaning back on his couch and raising his wine cup, "you are going to love it here. This island makes Boukos look like a jurist's funeral."

Hylas, on the other side of the governor's dining room, tried to smile as if that idea did not alarm him. Boukos, he had always been told, was a place of extreme decadence. And the island of Tykanos was worse? He clenched his fingers over the wet collection of olive pits in his palm and watched Loukianos drink. The man did not look decadent himself: his raised right arm was tanned and muscular, his greying blond hair further whitened by the sun. His high spirits seemed exaggerated, as bright as the colours in the frescos of his summer dining room.

"I–I will do my best to appreciate all that Tykanos has to offer," Hylas said seriously.

"Splendid!" Loukianos grinned at him. "I'll show you around all the tea houses myself."

"That is very kind of you, sir."

Hylas had heard of tea; it was a kind of eastern drink that

kept you awake. That did not sound very decadent either. He felt relief.

"Let me think," Loukianos went on. "Where should we start? There are six of them: the Jewels of Tykanos, that's what we call them. The Bower of Suos, that's my usual haunt, though some of my friends prefer the Amber Lily, and it does have its charms. We go to the Sunset Palace and the Peacock from time to time, because one has to, and Myrrha's is good for a laugh."

Hylas wasn't paying much attention to this. He was debating whether to put the olive pits in his hand on the table or drop them on the floor. He had accumulated so many of them now that he was concerned either action would call attention to itself. There were no empty dishes on the table, so he had been waiting to see what Loukianos would do, but Loukianos had not eaten any olives.

At home—in the place he tried not to think of as home anymore—Hylas would have spat the olive pits on the floor without a second thought. In Pheme, where he had lived for most of the last five years, the rules were more complicated, and you would get dirty looks when you discarded bones or pits or rinds in the wrong way.

"I'll take you to the Red Balconies," Loukianos was saying, "for the sake of completeness, and because it's the oldest house on Tykanos, though these days it's known mostly for its food and music."

Hylas nodded as if any of this made sense to him. So the tea houses also served food and hosted musical performances; he supposed that made sense.

"I am … I am sure it will be a pleasure to visit them all, sir," he said, "after working hard every day on your aqueduct."

"Excellent, excellent." Loukianos reached for the dish of olives. "Don't worry, you'll have plenty of spare time. Perhaps more than you'd like. There are always delays on this island.

Sourcing the stone, finding the labour." He spat an olive pit over his shoulder, making the gesture somehow elegant, like everything about him. "Negotiating with the Gylphians."

"Oh. Yes," said Hylas. He should have spat the pits after all. Damn. Now it was too late and he had to do something else with them. "There are always delays everywhere."

"Mm. Here especially. It's its own world, Tykanos." Loukianos gazed into the middle distance for a moment, then recovered his cheer and went on: "One of the things you'll realize quickly is that everyone on the island is from somewhere else. Gylphians, Sasians, Kossians, people from places you've never heard of. Myself, I'm Phemian enough to be appointed governor, but I've never lived more than a few years in the city of Pheme in my whole life."

"Is that so?" Hylas hoped this was not going to turn into an exchange of biographies where he would have to talk about his own upbringing.

But Loukianos was one of those people who was content to talk about himself. "I was born in the colonies," he said, "and grew up in my father's household moving around Sasia —he was an engineer like you, worked for the army. In my twenties I even spent some time in a royal household, one of the King of Sasia's palaces in the north-east. That was something! The gossip, the court intrigue, the forbidden women's quarters—it's all real, all much like the stories you hear. Went back to Pheme to further my career, as one does, and now— here I am. Come have a look around my gardens," he finished abruptly, swinging his legs down off the couch. "I've had them largely redone since moving into the governor's mansion."

Loukianos beckoned for a slave to bring his sandals, and Hylas tried to seize the moment to reach out and open his hand over the table. Several of the olive pits stuck to his palm, and he had to brush them off with his other hand. Loukianos saw what he was doing and gave him a quizzical

look, but he said nothing. Hylas felt his cheeks heating and
stood up stiffly, clenching his jaw.

As the six bells marking the middle of the day rang at the fort
down by the harbour, Hylas stood in the street outside the
governor's mansion. He had followed Loukianos on a long
tour of the gardens, looking at fishponds and shrubs and stat-
ues, wishing that he had any context at all for appreciating
such things. He wondered if forty was too old to learn.

He drew in a deep breath of the brisk sea air and let it
out, looking around him. The governor's mansion was at the
summit of Tykanos, in the enclave of rich men's houses that
capped the rocky peak rising above the beaches below. The
streets that he had climbed to get here from the harbour rose
steeply, broken in some places by steps, and he'd seen the
wealthy being carried by their slaves in chairs with long
handles.

He walked along the top of the wall that surrounded this
enclave, looking out over the island. To the north, he saw
vistas far out into the sparkling sea, all the places he'd lived so
far in his life hidden by distance. Coming around to the east,
there were forested hills. He'd seen Tykanos on a map, and
recalled that it was really a pair of islands, very close together
and joined by a causeway. That forest would be on the larger
of the two, if he had got his bearings right. Some of the trees
had turned colour, their leaves flame-orange against the back-
drop of the bright blue sea.

He kept walking and came around to the south side of
the summit. Here the coast of Gylphos was a dark line on the
horizon, the land in this area very flat. Hylas remembered
seeing that on the map, too. He leaned on the parapet of the
wall, his circuit of the summit completed, and looked down
at the harbour.

The fortifications that surrounded the harbour dominated the view. Hylas's gaze skittered away from their dark bulk. Beyond their walls, a long stone jetty ran out into the water, with several ships at anchor along it. Between the harbour and the residences of the upper slopes lay the small fortress town, with its pastel-coloured houses and shops, its water gardens and little avenues of painted statuary gleaming in the sun. It was beautiful; Hylas could understand why Loukianos loved it here.

He set off down the mountain in search of his lodgings. He'd been given directions and sent his sea chest on ahead while he went up to greet the governor immediately after arriving. Now he made his way to a shabby street nestled under the edge of the mountain road on the outskirts of the town, looking for a house with—he consulted the note in the letter he had brought with him—red balconies.

Hadn't Loukianos mentioned some place with red balconies? One of the tea houses—Hylas hoped he wouldn't really have to visit them all, though if he was to remain on good terms with the governor, he might. But surely the work on the aqueduct, a large and ambitious project, would keep him busy, even reckoning with the inefficiencies that might characterize island life.

The town was eclectic, as if it had been assembled from leftover bits of various cities. They must log the forest on the larger island, Hylas thought, because they seemed to build a lot in wood, more than he had seen in Pheme. Many of the houses had wooden balconies projecting from their upper storeys, shading the streets below.

He found the house he was looking for at the end of the street, right under the looming rock face of the mountain, which here was bare and sheer. The balconies, two of them on the house's upper storey, had beautifully constructed wooden railings, but their red paint was faded and peeling. The narrow entry hall was empty, the sun hot in the courtyard beyond, unrelieved by vegetation or the splashing of a fountain. There was a fountain, but it was as old as the rest of the house and quite dry.

It was a Sasian-style house, centred on the courtyard, with an arcade below and a gallery on the second-storey level, wooden like the balconies on the front. The proportions were pleasing, the space harmonious in spite of its age and air of neglect. You could see the mountain, its sheer cliffside stooping over the house, capped with a fringe of gnarled trees.

The haunting voice of a bowed instrument emanated from the shadows under the arcade on the opposite side of the courtyard, where a group of people lounged on cushions with small bowls in their hands. The musician was a young woman in an orange dress. She swayed with the motion of her bow, eyes closed.

Hylas looked around the courtyard uncertainly. Was this a lodging house? It didn't look particularly like any of the apartment buildings he had seen in Pheme, but then, he was far from Pheme here, in a town where the population was as mixed as the architecture. He stepped in under the arcade to get out of the sun, scanning the seated group to see if there was anyone who looked like a landlady.

There was a thin, olive-skinned woman of about his age, wearing a lot of gold bracelets, but she was asleep, leaning inelegantly on a cushion propped against the wall. Someone else, seeing Hylas and misunderstanding his intentions, kicked a spare cushion in his direction and waved indicatively at a spouted vessel and a stack of bowls on a small table. Hylas nodded with a spasmodic smile but did not move. He started to feel a ridiculous, rising panic. Was he in the wrong place? How was he going to find his lodgings?

A young woman noticed him after a moment and got to her feet, gathering up her heavy skirts.

"Welcome to the House of the Red Balconies, good sir,"

she murmured, stepping away from the musical group and making a startlingly graceful curtsey.

"Th-this is the Red Balconies?"

Was that not the name of the tea shop Loukianos had mentioned? The one that you visited only for the sake of completeness? The small bowls and the spouted vessel could certainly contain tea. But the place did not otherwise resemble a restaurant.

And he wasn't looking for a restaurant. He had been careful to arrange everything beforehand, writing to the agent whom Loukianos had recommended to secure lodgings in the town. He had followed the directions given in the agent's letter, but this was clearly the wrong place.

"Are you here to see anyone in particular?" the young woman asked with a smile. She had a pretty, heart-shaped face, and her hair was entirely concealed under an elaborately wrapped red scarf, balanced on top of her head like a big red flower.

Hylas cleared his throat. There was no need for panic. "Actually, I believe I may have mistaken the directions. I am new to the island. I'm looking for my lodgings."

"Oh, are you our new tenant?" Her manner changed just slightly, a fractional lowering of formality. "I did hear someone was coming."

"I ... really?"

"Oh yes." Her smile was now wide and genuine. "We're a tea house, but we have a spare apartment that we let out. It's quite nice. I can show you to it. What's your name?"

"Hylas Mnemotios." The surname was coming more readily to his lips now, feeling less like a lie. It was only a couple of months since he had started using it again.

"Nice to meet you, Hylas. I'm Taris. Follow me."

She padded away under the arcade, barefoot on the flag-stones. Hylas followed doubtfully.

"What are you doing on Tykanos?" she asked, glancing back over her shoulder.

That at least was an easy question to answer. "I am an engineer. I have been hired by Governor Loukianos to direct the building of a new aqueduct."

"Really?" She sounded delighted. "I'll have to introduce you to everyone—you'll be a sensation. The water situation in town is *quite* bad—I hear the aqueduct will be a tremendous improvement. It's certainly made Governor Loukianos very popular since he announced it."

Taris pulled aside a curtain in an arched doorway tucked in the very corner of the arcade, and Hylas followed her down a couple of steps into a small, dark, oddly shaped anteroom with bare walls and a flagged floor and two doors opening off it. She unlatched one of them and pushed it inward.

"Here you are," she said. "This is the apartment."

Hylas looked into the room, still half-sure this must all be a mistake. But no, it wasn't, because there under the window was the sea chest that he'd had sent ahead to his new lodgings.

"Ah," he said. "There are my things."

"Yes, we had the porter put them in here for you." Taris strode through the front room and opened an inner door. "There's two rooms, and a little courtyard at the back, which you share with Zo—and the bath you share with Zo and Chrestos, though you'll have to fetch and heat your own water, so you may prefer to go to the public baths. Our last tenant did. The one by the Sunset Palace is decent, I hear. The brand new one around the corner is usually closed, for some reason. And you're not allowed to use the girls' bath, so don't even ask." She laughed, but there was an edge to it which made him think that the last tenant *had* asked. "And you may want to buy some more furniture. Our last tenant took away everything that was in here when

8

he left, although it wasn't really his. We did our best to fix it up for you, but you may want some nicer things. I don't know if you'll find the bed big enough for you—you are tallish."

"It all appears perfectly satisfactory," said Hylas, as he would probably have said if she had shown him to a corner of a dirty stable instead of this airy, pleasant suite of rooms.

"Excellent." She headed back toward the outer door. "You get to take your meals with us, if you like, but if you want to take up any of the girls' time, you have to burn incense like everyone else."

"Of course," he said, since she was looking back at him as if expecting an answer, though he had no idea what she was talking about. "Where is the ... where is the tea sold?"

Taris's eyebrows went up. "What?"

It was obviously not the right question. He tried again. "I–I understand that this is a tea house ... "

"Oh, but we don't *sell* tea. That's just what it's called on the island. We're a house of companions. There's four of us girls, and Zo and Chrestos, though he's accepted a garland from Captain Themistokles."

Hylas felt an unpleasant sensation like being splashed with cold water. He had been misunderstanding this basic piece of vocabulary all morning. Of course when Loukianos talked about showing him around the island and said it made Boukos look tame, he hadn't been talking about places to buy tea.

"It's not going to be a problem, is it?" Taris lifted her chin slightly. Without waiting for an answer, she added, "You just pay us your rent every week, and we leave you to yourself. If you want anything else, you buy a stick of incense, and you get our company until it burns down—that's how it works for everyone, and you're not special just because you live here."

No doubt their last tenant, in between trying to use their

bath and stealing their furniture, had made a pest of himself in other ways.

"Of course," said Hylas forcefully. "It will certainly not be a problem."

Left alone, Hylas sat on the edge of the bed, looking down at his clasped hands. Life on Tykanos was going to be very different from what he had imagined.

He had seen himself, in his mind's eye, reporting occasionally to a busy and aloof governor, directing a crew of subordinates, and otherwise spending his time alone, returning after long days of work to a solitary room in some lodging house where he would trouble no one, talk to no one, and no one need know how thin a veneer of civilization he had acquired even after five years.

Instead of that, Loukianos was a gregarious person who obviously didn't have enough work to do and looked on his newly hired engineer as a potential friend, and the lodgings were in a pleasure house where he was expected to have communal meals with companions. The work seemed likely to proceed in fits and starts, so he would be spending some of his time touring other pleasure houses and meeting other companions with Loukianos. Companions, who were renowned for their wit and sophistication, who could recite poetry and probably expected you to be able to recite poetry back at them, or at least to know whether or not to spit olive pits on the floor.

There were probably some men—there were certainly *plenty* of men—who would find this whole situation enviable. Hylas wished he could trade places with one of them.

Well, he had been hired to build an aqueduct, not to be a drinking buddy for the governor, and surely he wouldn't lose the job just because he wasn't very good company. He would finish the work and move on. If he disgraced himself, it would not be for the first time, and if he had to pick himself up and repair the damage and carry on as best he could, it would not be the first time for that either.

He got up from the bed and went to slide open the lattice screen that covered the door to the courtyard at the back of his apartment. His first thought, as he looked out, was that they should have been charging twice as much rent. The "courtyard" was a small formal garden tucked in between the corner of the tea house and the bare limestone of the cliff face. A high wooden fence, its red paint weathered like the balconies on the front, closed off the space on the left-hand side. On the right, the house was built right up to the cliff, as if it had emerged or been carved from it. Another lattice-screened doorway in that wall stood half-open to admit the breeze.

In the middle of the lawn was a gnarled old olive tree. Around the edge was a gravel path, lined with plants of different kinds that Hylas couldn't identify. A row of neatly trimmed ornamental trees in pots stood along the fence. Someone had started building a dry stone wall—rather slop-pily—under the cliff, perhaps with an eye to making a terraced section of the garden, a clever idea. There were heaps of stone and earth, overgrown with weeds, as if work had been suspended for a few months. The lawn needed atten-tion, too—Hylas didn't think the ragged plants poking up in places were meant to be part of the effect. Still, it was a beau-tifully planned space.

Fresh from his tour of Governor Loukianos's garden, Hylas felt newly equipped to appreciate this one. It was a Sasian formal garden in miniature, the layout and propor-tions reflecting something to do with Sasian cosmology that Loukianos had not explained very clearly. He had wanted to make his own garden over in this style, he'd told Hylas, but had been hampered by its pre-existing features. Whoever designed this garden had been able to commit to the design scheme much more fully. The air carried the scent of rosemary.

Hylas walked around the garden, following the gravel path, taking the long route to arrive at the other door. Thinking to introduce himself to his neighbour, he looked tentatively inside.

There was a couch just inside the door, and a young man was sleeping on it. He lay half curled up in the shadows, his long blue robe covering his feet but open at the throat, his sleeping face soft with repose. The green glass beads of his earrings glittered in the spill of black hair over the cushions.

Hylas took a step backward, startled. This person's beauty, glimpsed in the dimness of the room, seemed of a piece with the hidden garden, surprising and almost magical.

He had better manners than to stare at a sleeping woman, but the opportunity to stare at a beautiful young man in his sleep had somehow never arisen. Of course, there were reasons not to do that, too.

A bird cawed on the mountain above them, a long, raucous sound, and the sleeper woke with a start. Suddenly in motion, sweeping back loose hair with a long-fingered hand, draperies shifting around a supple figure as he sat forward into the sunlight, he looked out at Hylas.

His narrow eyes were as black as his hair, their depths emphasized with smoky kohl. His skin was fawn-coloured under a dusting of paler powder, his cheekbones high and broad, his lips full. His eyebrows, perfect black slashes, rose unsmilingly.

"Were you looking for me?" he said.

"N-n-no." How could he have been, when he hadn't known such a person belonged to the waking world?

"Then … " the young man prompted impatiently. He had a voice as dark as his eye-makeup, inflected by some accent that was a complete mystery to Hylas.

"I … was looking at the garden."

The young man gave this explanation the unimpressed look it deserved. "How did you get in?"

"Through the … " Hylas twisted to point vaguely behind him. Finally it occurred to him what detail was lacking here. "Through my apartment. I'm the new tenant."

"You're the new tenant. I see."

He relaxed slightly, and only then did Hylas realize that his pose as he sat on the bed had been full of tension. He had, of course, been alarmed to wake up and find someone looking at him; he'd just done a good job of hiding it.

"I—I'm sorry, I—"

"Fortunate meeting," the young man cut him off brusquely, with a little gesture that suggested this was a formulaic greeting. "I'm Zo."

Hylas saw that he wasn't going to be allowed to apologize for scaring his neighbour. Fair enough.

"I see," he said instead. "Are you—I mean, I am Hylas." He cleared his throat. "Hylas. Are you—also—a tenant?"

"No. I am one of the Red Balconies' companions."

"Oh!" That meant, if he had understood Taris's explanation, that he needed to buy a stick of incense or something before starting a conversation? "Then I'd better … I mean … " What was he saying? "I am honoured by your acquaintance." By some miracle he got out a whole, coherent sentence. "I will not take up any more of your time."

"God guard your coming and your going," said Zo, the foreign greeting perfectly polite, the dryness inescapable.

Hylas fled; there was no other word for it. He got back into his own bedroom and slid the lattice shut behind him. He paced around the room. What had Taris said about the bath? He was to share it with Zo and someone else, perhaps another equally daunting person. He would certainly be going to the public bath house.

CHAPTER 2

So THEY'D RENTED the vacant apartment again after all. Zo slouched in the chair at his dressing table and lifted his hand mirror, looking up at himself from a novel angle. He looked all right, makeup and jewellery relatively undisturbed by napping in the middle of the day. He'd readied himself earlier than usual that day because Djosi had said he might come by in the afternoon, and he didn't want to be caught unprepared. He had hopes of Djosi.

The man next door complicated things there. He'd have to explain to Djosi that the garden wasn't really private anymore.

Thinking about that made him tired again, and he eyed his bed wistfully. The nap hadn't been long enough. Naps never were.

He hoped the new tenant wasn't going to be trouble like the last man. Coming home drunk and bothering the girls, leaving garbage in the anteroom, relieving himself in Zo's garden … Zo really hadn't wanted the place rented again. It had been nice having the whole corner of the house to himself. A bit lonely, but it was better than the alternative.

Angels of the Almighty, he was another Pseuchaian man,

the new tenant; was Zo going to have to beg and cajole him to use the privy instead of shitting in the garden like a dog? Was it something they all did? He didn't know.

He dropped the mirror onto his table with a clatter and ran his hand through his hair. To be fair, the new tenant made a better first impression than the old one had. He might be a bit tongue-tied, but there was something appealing about him: a gentleness in his eyes, an unsmiling kindness, as if he was diligently looking for good in everything he saw. The previous man hadn't had any of that.

The new man had had the misfortune to catch Zo when he'd just woken after an inadequate nap on a bad pain day, so Zo had been surly to him. He wasn't proud of that; he could usually keep better control over his mask, even when he was feeling bad. But he'd been startled, too—it was probably understandable.

He'd wait and see what this Hylas was like before he decided how to proceed. Maybe the fact that he'd started off their interaction by being less than charming would ultimately prove useful. Sometimes it did.

Hylas's second morning on Tykanos was spent at the government office next to the fort, trying to find someone who knew anything about the aqueduct project. Was there money allocated to it, were there other people assigned to it besides himself, did it in fact exist in any form other than as a promise made to the town by the governor of the island?

It was only with the arrival of the governor himself, around the sixth hour, that some notes were unearthed outlining in the most general terms where the aqueduct was proposed to go and what it was expected to accomplish. There were two water sources proposed: one on the smaller island, which barely needed an aqueduct to get water down to the town; the other on the larger island, which would mean building out across the water, a much more significant job.

"This looks promising," said Hylas, sitting at Loukianos's desk—at Loukianos's insistence—and studying the documents. Not that there was much to study, and calling it "promising" was being generous. Still, he was here to work.

"First I will need to assemble a team to help me survey the two sites," he went on. "Perhaps I can borrow men from the fort? They should have experienced surveyors there."

"Mm." Loukianos leaned on the corner of his desk and looked critically at his manicured nails. "Mutari is the person to talk to about that."

"Mu … tari." Hylas made a note of the name in the wax tablet he had brought with him. "He is the chief engineer at the fort?"

"What?" Loukianos looked confused. "No, no—Mutari's the mistress of the naval quartermaster. She'll get it sorted out for you."

Hylas stared at him. Were they somehow not talking about the same thing?

"I have to talk to the quartermaster's mistress in order to get a survey team?"

Loukianos nodded as if he didn't see anything odd about it. "If you want help from the fort, yes. You have to approach them in the right way—they get their hackles up about the strangest things—but Mutari's very good. Unfortunately, I believe she's still over in Gylphos, visiting her sister."

"Oh." That stymied Hylas, who had expected simply to walk into the fort and ask to speak to the proper authorities. Not that he'd been looking forward to that; it would be a relief not to have to do it, in fact. "Well, I'll … I could ride out and take a look at the springs myself. That would be a start."

"Right, good. I'll have my man Niko look you up some

decent horseflesh—no mean feat on this island, let me tell you, but Niko is simply the best. I don't keep a stable myself, alas. But Niko should have something for you in a couple of days. As soon as I can find him. I'm not sure … Well, he's around somewhere, it's not a big island." He laughed easily.

Hylas opened his mouth to speak and then closed it without saying anything. Would he lose face if he admitted that he had intended to hire a mule from a place he'd seen near the harbour and go that afternoon?

"Now," Governor Loukianos went on, "the reason I came by was to make sure you got some spending money. Will three hundred or so do you, do you think?"

Hylas made an effort not to let his mouth drop open soundlessly again. He couldn't think what to say. *Three hundred what?* Phemian nummoi, presumably, as that must be the official currency of the island, but surely that was a huge sum? A discussion of salary had been notably absent from the negotiations over this job, and he had taken that to mean that it wouldn't pay well, which hadn't bothered him. His needs were few. But three hundred nummoi? How often was he to be paid that? Monthly? *Weekly?* Before he saw the governor's palace and garden, he wouldn't have imagined it possible, but now …

"P-perfectly, yes, sir."

Loukianos pushed off from the desk. "I'll have them get it ready for you tomorrow. So there's nothing else to be done today, and you'll be able to join me at the Sunset Palace." He rubbed his hands together with satisfaction. "Excellent. I'm looking forward to introducing you to everyone."

Hylas got home late. He was glad that the walk from the Sunset Palace to the House of the Red Balconies was short, just a couple of dark streets separating the two tea houses. He had drunk more than usual—wine, not tea—and though he was still clear-headed, he was tired and wanted nothing more than to fall into his bed.

The Sunset Palace had been much as he expected, a beautiful building full of beautiful women who tried to make him feel welcome and special. It wasn't their fault that they failed so badly. It wasn't Loukianos's fault either. He had been attentive enough, introducing Hylas to all the companions and the other guests, making sure Hylas's cup was always full and giving him no opportunity to slip away unnoticed. If it had been in Hylas's power to enjoy such an evening, he would presumably have had a good time.

He hadn't. It had been like the olive pits in the governor's dining room all over again, magnified into a whole evening of not knowing what to do, what to say when anyone spoke to him, where to look or how to position his body so that he looked like someone who felt at ease. Whenever anyone looked at him, he thought he could feel their scepticism. "What's he doing here?" he could imagine them asking. He wanted to tell them he didn't know either.

The House of the Red Balconies was almost unrecognizable after dark. Light glowed from the courtyard out into the entry hall, and music and voices enlivened the interior. The sleepy air of the daytime was gone, the shabbiness of the courtyard hidden by shadows.

Hylas spotted Taris, the companion he had met first, sitting in the courtyard with a group of men around her. This evening her headscarf was gold, still wrapped like an elaborate flower. The woman he assumed was the mistress of the house, the one with all the bracelets, was greeting guests as they arrived. He started to hasten across the courtyard toward his rooms, when it occurred to him that he might still be mistaken for a guest, being unknown to most of the companions, and he should introduce himself to the woman in charge.

He lingered while the mistress spoke with the men who had just entered. His gaze wandered to the gallery above the arcade around the courtyard, and he saw a door open and a group of guests and companions come out, talking boisterously. Among them was the young man Hylas had seen sleeping, Zo. He was laughing elegantly and leaning on the arm of a tall man with a bald head, as if he needed assistance to walk. The group disappeared through another doorway, and the mistress of the house was greeting Hylas and asking him something.

"Did I see you noticing our Zo?" she repeated, giving him an indulgent smile. "Let me take you up to join his party."

"Oh. No. Er, I'm not—I'm the new tenant."

The mistress's manner immediately changed. "What do you want, then?"

"Nothing. Just to tell you that. I'm on my way to bed."

She rolled her eyes. "Nice to be like you," she muttered as she turned away.

"Did your man Djosi end up going home?" Chrestos asked with a yawn as he and Zo were closing up the upstairs sitting room for the night.

"Yes," said Zo. "He was here all afternoon, though."

"Ooh. How did that go?"

Zo shrugged. "Honestly, not very well. I think I made a misstep, telling him the garden wouldn't be private anymore now that there's a new tenant."

"Well, that's true. What was wrong with that?"

"He thought it meant I wanted to do something private in the garden."

Chrestos snickered.

"I mean, I *did*. I guess that's not his thing."

"Well, now you know."

They were out in the gallery by this time, closing the door behind them.

"Do you want me to get Ahmos to carry you downstairs?" Chrestos asked cheerfully.

"I'll be fine," said Zo, smiling, instead of growling or snapping at Chrestos, because he'd conserved enough energy not only to get down the stairs by himself but to be gracious about it. He felt proud of himself.

The following morning, Hylas dragged himself out of bed and went in search of tea. It helped you wake up, he'd heard. And this was nominally a tea house, so they must keep the stuff on hand somewhere. Two days before, in searching for the privy, he had found the kitchen at the back of the house, so he headed there now.

"You're the aqueduct man, aren't you?" the cook said when he presented himself. She called to one of her subordinates: "Tea for the aqueduct man, Dria!"

"Hello, aqueduct man!" called the cook's assistant.

Hylas leaned against the worktable while he waited. In his wandering the other day he had also found the cistern that supplied bath water for the house, and learned that drinking water had to be brought from the public fountain down the street.

"Has the fountain in the courtyard been dry a long time?" he asked.

"Five or six years," the cook said. "We tried to get the landlord to fix it, but then the water on this whole street failed, so it wouldn't matter, even if he could be bothered."

"You mean other buildings on the street used to have piped water, and now it doesn't work?"

"As far as I know. That fountain at the end of the street's

fed by a different source altogether, that's why it's still flowing."

"I see." So the aqueduct was going to help, but only if other repairs were made to the water delivery system of the town. Hylas wondered whether that was part of Governor Loukianos's plan too.

A woman came in lugging a jar of oil and struggling to suppress laughter.

"Guess who I just saw leaving?" she said, elbowing the cook.

"Captain Themistokles," the cook's assistant guessed.

"What? No, Captain Themistokles—I've stopped even *noticing* him, he's like a part of the furniture. No, it was Gordios. The spice merchant?"

"No! Who was he with?" the cook demanded.

"He was by himself when I saw him, and he didn't look happy to be alive. I think he got drunk in a corner and slept here, and nobody noticed."

"Gods, I wonder if he did! How comical!"

"It won't be if it gets talked about," the cook's assistant put in drearily from where she was working at the stove. "You think the girls here *want* this to be the kind of house where drunks fall asleep in corners? You go to the cheap wine shops and the brothels down by the harbour for that."

"True enough," said the cook with a sigh.

"Oh, hello," said the oil-carrier, finally noticing Hylas. "Who are you?"

"He's the new tenant, the aqueduct man."

"Oh, the aqueduct man! Don't pay any attention to what I was just saying, sir."

"He's just had to come to the kitchen to get his own tea," the cook's assistant intoned. "I think he knows we're a house fallen on hard times."

"Oh, not at all, I mean I—that's—it's no trouble."

Mercifully, the tea was ready by this time. The cook's

assistant brought over a small clay pot, its handle wrapped in a cloth, with steam rising from the spout, and the cook placed it on a tray with a basket of fresh buns and two little glazed bowls, then handed the whole thing to Hylas. He didn't know whether the two bowls were because she expected him to share the tea with someone or because there was some other, mysterious use for the second bowl. Did tea have pits that you had to spit out? He thanked her, nodded politely to all three women, and left the kitchen.

He took the tray back to his apartment and set it on the floor, since there was no table. He thought fleetingly of going out into the private yard, but the prospect of running into his neighbour again frightened him, so he settled down inside.

He plumped down a cushion, in imitation of the people he had seen sitting in the courtyard, and lifted the lid of the pot with the cloth to peer inside. Something crumbled and dark was floating in the water, which had turned a clear amber. Were you supposed to fish that out? Was that what the second bowl was for? But surely a spoon or something would have been more useful.

He replaced the lid and poured some tea into one of the bowls. The pot had a strainer built into the spout, his discovered, so few of the solids came out. Hylas blew on the surface of the tea and sipped gingerly. It was very hot, with an earthy, slightly bitter flavour that was completely different than he had expected. He liked it.

CHAPTER 3

THE MORNING POT of tea and basket of buns became a daily thing. Hylas learned the name of the cook—Elpis—and some of her assistants—Gio, Tuma, and Dria—and their opinion of the landlord (very low) and the mistress of the Red Balconies (not much higher).

"She's a harpy," was Gio's judgement.

"She likes things to look just so," in Dria's more nuanced view, "and she takes it to extremes. That's why she quarrelled with young Zo last winter."

They always gave Hylas two bowls with his tea and more buns than he could eat in one sitting, and he never protested or explained that he had no one to share them with.

He took his breakfast in the back garden now, under the looming cliff face in the shade of the olive tree. He had realized that all the inhabitants of the Red Balconies slept late, so there was no likelihood of encountering his neighbour at this hour. He would drink as much of the tea as he comfortably could, eat half of the buns—they were delicious, stuffed with different fillings, some sweet and some savoury—and wrap the rest up in a cloth to take with him to work.

Not that he was doing much work. He was trying: he had

hired the mule and gone out, a couple of days in a row, to survey the site on the little island as best he could by himself, but much of it was impassable scrubland, and you needed a team to do it properly. The site on the big island was apparently even worse. He'd asked around at the government office and learned the name of the navy's chief surveyor, but everyone seemed to agree that they'd need to wait until the quartermaster's mistress returned from Gylphos before actually requesting his help. He hadn't gone down to the fort.

The three hundred nummoi had duly materialized on the second morning, and the staff of the government office had been helpful in suggesting how much of it he might want to keep at home and explaining how to deposit the greater portion with the treasurers at the Temple of Amphiaraos in the town's small agora. He'd got through that procedure with a minimum amount of embarrassment, and to celebrate had gone out to the market and treated himself to a few luxuries.

Eventually, to keep himself busy and avoid spending another afternoon trying to appreciate Governor Loukianos's gardens, he had set himself a project of checking the map of water sources in the town and its environs. The people in the governor's office clearly thought he was wasting his time doing this, as the existing map, which was painted on the wall of the government office, was wonderfully detailed, with artistic renderings of the various fountains and wells in their locations. Hylas mumbled something apologetic about needing to see things with his own eyes and agreed that the map was indeed a thing of beauty. On his first day comparing the map to the streets of the town, he found that the map was inaccurate, had been inaccurate when it was first painted, and was now out of date, showing fountains that were no longer in use and omitting at least one major well. So he was discreetly drafting a new one, much less distinguished artistically, but much more accurate.

His evenings were spent with Governor Loukianos and

his friends at the tea houses. His afternoons could have been spent there too, and sometimes were, if he made the mistake of being somewhere where the governor could find him at around the time the tea houses opened, and not appearing adequately busy.

Afternoons were the times when the tea houses actually served tea, and the atmosphere was relaxed and, in some ways, more intimate, because there were fewer guests. It might have suited Hylas better, but in fact it put him intolerably on edge; there were no crowds or shadows to hide in, no one was lit up with drink or distracted by dancers, and everyone looked you in the eye. People really did expect you to recite poetry in the afternoons. Evenings, when you could pretend to be a sleepy drunk, or enraptured by a performance, or just very busy eating, were easier.

So far, Loukianos and his friends, with Hylas in their wake, had visited only three of the Jewels of Tykanos: the Sunset Palace, the largest of all the houses; the Bower of Suos, Loukianos's favourite, where about half of the companions were boys and very young men, and the wine tasted like something that should be poured over cake; and the Amber Lily, Hylas's least favourite, where the food was scanty and the poetry almost non-stop, which they had visited more than either of the others because one of Loukianos's friends was in love with a woman there.

You didn't pay for your drinks or your food at the tea houses; you just bought a stick of incense and settled in until it burned down and someone came to ask discreetly if you'd like to pay for another one. And, in fact, Hylas never paid for his own; Loukianos always paid for him, or rather added him to his tab, since the governor seemed to have an account running at all the houses they had visited. Hylas might have protested at this if he had been enjoying these evenings more. He felt guilty when he thought about all that money at the Temple of Amphiaraos, but a lifelong habit of frugality reminded him to be grateful he wasn't having to spend whatever an evening at the tea houses cost—because the governor didn't actually pay, he had no idea—every night of the week. And he wasn't going to be paid three hundred nummoi every week, either; he'd realized that after the first week ended and no new bag of coins appeared. It must be a monthly salary, which was something of a relief.

The town itself was small, and all the permanent residents knew each other and were well informed on each other's business. The fort, when fully garrisoned, housed a population larger than the town, of marines stationed on Tykanos and legionaries waiting to be sent on to other posts. The sailors themselves were another, ever-shifting population, and there were merchants who came and went regularly. And then there were people who came simply to visit, from Pheme and Boukos and Gylphos, because the tea houses of Tykanos, long a well-kept secret of the sailors and traders and marines, were beginning to be talked about in the cities. It was changing the island; everyone seemed to agree on that. Most people thought it was changing for the better.

"We used to get pirates," Elpis said in the kitchen one morning. "I remember when we used to get pirates."

"It wasn't that long ago," Dria pointed out. "It's only two years since the Dodeki were put down."

"Yes, but they weren't coming as much even before that. I remember the days when somebody would spot a sail in the harbour and run through the streets yelling 'Lock your doors!'"

A few of the people Hylas met seemed to think the change was for the worse.

"The threat of piracy was always greatly overstated," the governor's neighbour Timon said dismissively when someone brought it up one evening at the Amber Lily. "All kinds of ships dock in the harbour, and some of them may have been pirates in the past, but they weren't doing any harm—they could hardly get up to much, with the naval presence on this island."

"You liked the pirates because they were good for business," another of the governor's friends scoffed.

Timon didn't try to deny it. He was a merchant whose shop specialized in selling expensive swords and armour to the marines and the soldiers at the fort. He had a contract to supply the navy with the bronze used to make the rams on warships.

"If you were to dredge up the wrecks of those Dodeki ships they sank in the harbour at Pheme, you'd find more than a few weapons from my shop—all paid for, I might add. But that's not why I miss the pirates. The fact is, this town was livelier when it had a bit of an edge to it. Rawer. More real. Like a woman when she wants you but is also just a little afraid of you."

"As if he has any idea what that's like," Loukianos whispered to Hylas.

He might not have, Hylas thought, but he liked the sound of it, and that was bad enough.

The part of the night Hylas enjoyed most was coming home. The Red Balconies would be lit up, appearing at its best, strange and off-limits and yet welcoming. He would slink in the doors, ignored by the mistress now, exchanging a courteous nod or a greeting with Ahmos, the bouncer, if he was on duty. There would be other familiar faces in the courtyard and the arcade as he passed through; he had met most of the companions during the day, in passing, and was known to them as "the aqueduct man," so he would smile discreetly and return a wave or two.

There was Menthe, a young woman with wavy auburn hair and beautiful blue eyes; Pani, with black hair in ringlets and a Gylphian accent; and Theano, older than the others, pale-complexioned and black-haired and seemingly second in command to Mistress Aula. The kitchen day staff, who were the only ones Hylas had much conversation with, would be gone to bed long ago, in order to rise early and begin the next day's baking.

He never exchanged smiles or greetings with Zo, although he saw him most nights. Zo seemed to have a devoted circle of admirers; Hylas spotted the same men with him more than once. Sometimes he would be with only one of them, or part of a larger group with many different companions and guests. He was always smiling when Hylas saw him at night, smiling or laughing or listening with rapt and pleasant attention to something one of his guests was saying. Hylas continued to find the whole idea of him frightening.

Zo played the flute, or some foreign instrument that resembled a flute and whose sound moved Hylas almost to tears the one time that he heard Zo playing in the courtyard. He dressed in long, enfolding robes and wore earrings and kohl around his eyes, much like the other companions. When he walked, he always leaned on someone; other times, Hylas would see him being carried by Ahmos or by one of his guests.

One night, Hylas returned home especially late from the Amber Lily, where he had listened uncomfortably to Loukianos's friend trying to win a battle of wits against his beloved. The courtyard was mostly empty, and he had the idea of going to the kitchen to see if there were any leftovers that they might be willing to give him, as he was hungry. He returned to his room juggling a pitcher of wine and pieces of bread and cheese that had been pressed upon him by the night cook.

The door of Zo's room opened as Hylas was trying to get his own door unlatched without setting down his burdens. A tall, dark-skinned man slipped out; Hylas recognized him as one of Zo's regular guests. He turned in the doorway, and Hylas caught snatches of murmured speech against his will: "

... cruel that we must ... " " ... again as soon as ... " " ... exquisite ... " Gods, what was wrong with this damned door? He saw nothing of Zo except his delicate hands, which his departing lover was clasping. The latch of his door gave way finally and he all but fell inside.

Zo went upstairs himself in the morning to knock on Chrestos's door. He was feeling good after his night with Djosi—not a given, by any means. Sometimes sex left him aching and unable to move the next day, even if it had been good in the moment. Sometimes it helped him relax, and this seemed to have been one of those times. He was debating whether Djosi would want to hear that or not—he didn't know the man very well yet—as he climbed the stairs.

Chrestos had one of the rooms on the front of the house with a balcony, one of the famous formerly red balconies that the house was named after. The other balconies belonged to public sitting rooms and Mistress Aula's own apartment, so it was a particular privilege for Chrestos to have one. It was on account of his loyal patron, of course.

Captain Themistokles himself answered the door when Zo knocked, looking pristine and military and not at all as if he had just rolled out of his boyfriend's bed.

"Good morning," he said. "Chrestos is not up yet. Would you like me to wake him?"

"No need. I just came to see if I could borrow back a razor I loaned him a while ago. It's got a lily carved on the handle—I don't suppose you've seen it?"

"Seen it—I used it this morning." Themistokles rubbed his clean-shaven chin reflexively. "I'd no idea it was yours. Chrestos has had that for donkey's ages."

"Well, I don't need it often." Zo smiled wryly. None of

the men from his homeland could grow much of a beard—
and trying to follow Zashian fashions, they all tried.

"Must be nice," Themistokles remarked. "Let me get you
the razor and sharpen it for you."

Zo lounged in the doorway while Chrestos's patron
fetched the razor and gave it a few strokes on a whetstone
which he for some reason had with him. All the while
Chrestos slept, or pretended to sleep; Zo could see his shape
under the blankets beyond a half-drawn curtain over the
sleeping alcove at the side of the room. As he was leaving, he
heard Themistokles's loud voice from the alcove: "Come on,
stir yourself! We're going shopping, I'm going to buy you a
razor."

There was no denying that Zo envied Chrestos. What
would it be like to have a patron like that, so straightforwardly a part of your life that he answered your door while
you were asleep and treated your things like his own? Though
perhaps Themistokles thought of Chrestos's things as his own
because he paid for them. He might think of Chrestos as his
property too, and that would be less pleasant. He was a good
man—Zo had never heard anything to the contrary—but
one still didn't want to feel owned.

On his way down the stairs back to his room, he heard
voices below. Taris was gossiping with someone in the anteroom outside Zo's door, and Zo had a pretty good idea who
it must be. Why would she have been in that corner of the
house except to see him or his neighbour? He stopped on the
stairs, silent out of old habit, to hear what she was saying.

"I guess you could say the house has fallen on hard times.
We're certainly not as happy here as we used to be."

"Oh," said the person she was talking to, lamely. Yes, it
was certainly Zo's neighbour.

"I'd say it's been about a year," Taris went on
unprompted. "Since around the time Theano had her baby,
or maybe before that, when Hippolytos died. And the roof

30

had to be redone. Not that those things had anything to do with each other, but they were both blows, coming almost one on top of the other, and it left us struggling. The winter's always a harder time anyway, with fewer guests. And Theano had a difficult pregnancy and a worse birth."

"Oh dear. That … that must have frightened everyone."

Zo eased himself carefully down to sit on the steps. He wasn't particularly surprised to hear Taris talking to the new tenant like this; she was a chatty person who liked talking to men more than she liked actively flirting with them. But he wanted to hear how she would tell this story. Likely he wanted to hear it more than the aqueduct man himself did; he'd sounded uncomfortable, to Zo's mind.

"It did. And honestly, Mistress has been in a funk for a long time. Pani and Menthe say it's because she didn't want Theano to keep the baby, but *I* don't think that's true. She did quarrel with Zo, though—that's true, we all heard that."

Ah, there it was. Eavesdrop long and well enough and you'd always hear someone talking about you; that had been true in Rataxa, and apparently it was true here too.

"Oh," said Hylas again, and could Taris not *tell* that he wanted none of this information?

She couldn't, or she didn't care; she went on: "I think it was a misunderstanding—she wasn't trying to be mean, but she has a harsh way of saying things sometimes. And between you and me, I don't think she knows how to deal with male companions. They're kind of betwixt and between, you know?"

"I—I—Are they?"

He doesn't know, Zo thought; he doesn't pay any attention to us. He barely paid attention to the women, from what Zo could see.

"Anyway," Taris was saying, "Zo used to be much more sociable before that—I mean, he's sociable with the guests still, he comes out of his room and is quite dazzling all night, then he goes back and shuts himself up in his corner of the house and hardly comes out during the day. It's a shame. He used to help us with our wool-work during the day, you know? He got Pani and Menthe to teach him to spin, and he was getting quite decent at it. I thought it was sweet of him. You'd never catch Chrestos doing that!"

All right, that was enough. Zo got to his feet and was about to begin noisily descending the stairs.

"He … he must really want to be one of you," the aqueduct man said, and Zo froze again. He hadn't said that in the way Zo would have expected; it hadn't been a scoff or even a cringing "Oh, how … *nice*." It had sounded earnest.

"Well, perhaps he did, at the time," Taris allowed.

"What was the quarrel about?"

"Oh, it was … " She'd succeeded in getting him interested in the subject, and now she didn't want to talk about it anymore, clearly. "I probably shouldn't be gossiping like this. Let's get these into your room, and then I should go finish my chores."

"I—I can take that, you needn't—"

Taris laughed brightly. "Of course you can, it's not as if you need me carrying things for you, is it? Sorry for talking your ear off. It's just nice to have a new face around here who's not a guest, you know?"

The aqueduct man mumbled something polite, and Taris handed over whatever it was they had been bringing to his room—linens or something, maybe, to replace the things Pantaleon had taken with him when he left—and after a moment Zo heard a door shutting and silence. He went quietly down the stairs himself and into his own room.

He often woke with the sun and lay in bed trying pointlessly to get back to sleep, so he'd heard the new tenant out in the garden, and knew he'd developed a habit of taking his breakfast under the olive tree. That was certainly better than what Pantaleon had used the garden for. One more point in the aqueduct man's favour.

"I think I'll stay in tonight," Hylas told Governor Loukianos, two weeks after beginning his job. "I'm afraid I need a rest."

"Of course, of course!" Loukianos agreed indulgently. "I've been running you ragged, keeping you out until all hours of the night. And you're a man of sober habits, I should have known it by looking at you. Timon said as much."

Hylas felt a perverse need to argue that Timon hadn't judged him correctly, even though he clearly had, and probably "sober habits" was much more flattering than what he had actually said. Whatever it was, no doubt it was deserved.

"It is true," Hylas said, instead of arguing. "I have not got the stamina that all of you have."

He returned home feeling rather pleased with himself, as if an evening alone was a prize he had won. He fetched water from the cistern and took a cold, brisk bath, a habit retained from his early life. As it turned out, he had not been bothering with the public bath. Dressed in a clean tunic, he made his way back to his room.

A young man he'd never seen before stood on the dark landing, thumping a fist on the door next to Hylas's.

"Zo, come *on*!" he groaned. "Why are you *taking* so long?"

Hylas hesitated, not wanting to call attention to himself by slipping past to his own door, but also not wishing to be caught standing there awkwardly, with damp hair and a bundle of dirty clothes, when Zo opened the door. If Zo was going to open the door.

It was too late, anyway, as the young man at the door had

noticed him and turned to stare, then look him up and down, wide-eyed.

"Immortal gods, are you the aqueduct man?" he exclaimed.

He was a youth of about twenty, nearly Hylas's height, with broad, square shoulders and almost exaggeratedly slim hips. His hair was a mass of bright gold curls, piled up and tied with a ribbon in such a way that they spilled over his forehead. He had pearl-white skin and a profile you could have used to cut gemstones.

"Yes," said Hylas, "that's me. You must be Chrestos."

"I am! How did you know?"

"A lucky guess," said Hylas. But really, who else could this young man have been?

"Everyone's been talking about you," Chrestos confided. "It's been driving me *mad* that I haven't met you."

"H-have they? What have they been saying?"

"That you're building an aqueduct that's going to get the water flowing all over Tykanos. Is it true?"

"W-well, I'm an engineer, I'm directing the project, not actually building it by hand."

Chrestos laughed boisterously as if that had been a very good joke. "I heard you haven't burned incense in the evening with us yet, and all the girls are *longing* to get to know you better. Of course *I'm* usually busy in the evenings myself. I have an exclusive patron? Captain Themistokles. He takes up *all* of my time."

"I see," said Hylas politely. "I'm new to the island, so I'm afraid I don't know who that is."

The companion looked surprised and pleased, and Hylas realized he'd inadvertently paid him a compliment in assuming his patron was famous. It seemed a good moment to make his escape.

"If you'll excuse me," he said finally, sidling past to reach his own door. "It, uh, was nice to meet you."

CHAPTER 4

"I FINALLY MET THE AQUEDUCT MAN," Chrestos reported proudly when Zo opened his door.

Zo leaned on the doorframe and adjusted his grip on his crutch. "Congratulations? I hope that isn't what you've been hammering on my door to tell me."

"No, of course not. I met him just now, while I was waiting *forever* for you to answer your door. Mistress wants us all dressed in our best in the courtyard by sunset. There's some sort of dignitary coming."

"Fine," said Zo, nodding curtly. "I'll be there."

"Obviously you'll have to leave the stick behind. Why've you got it now, anyway? We all thought you were getting better."

This rankled Zo more than all the rest. Chrestos had known him for a year—the others longer.

"I get better and then I get worse again, Chrestos," he growled. "That's the way it works. I hope Mistress knows if she wants me not to use my crutch, she'd better send Ahmos to carry me."

"I'll tell him," said Chrestos.

Zo shrugged. "If you feel like it. See you at sunset."

And he closed the door.

His bed felt very far away, but it was also the only destination in the room that interested him. He resisted the urge to sink down and sit on the floor; that, he knew from experience, would only create a new and harder task of getting up.

A few months ago, during a period when he'd been feeling better than usual, the tide of pain and fatigue temporarily gone far out, he'd had the idea to put a bunch of pegs on the wall and hang his clothes and jewellery so that he could see everything without having to dig through chests or boxes. He'd bought another chair to add to his collection—he had three others, one by his bed, one at his desk, and one out in his garden—so that he could sit down to dress.

It made the room look odd, which would become a problem if he ever acquired a patron whom he wanted to entertain privately. But for now that possibility seemed pretty remote, and the way he'd arranged his room let him carry on with his life in reasonable comfort.

It was funny how taken everyone was with the aqueduct man. Zo was apparently the last of the companions to have a conversation with him. And yet he must have been one of the first to meet him, the day that he arrived, and his room was next door to the aqueduct man's, sharing access to the back courtyard.

Zo picked out a robe and sat in his chair to dress, then moved to his desk where he sat to put on his makeup, and finally sat in the chair by his bed to look out at his garden, waiting for sunset. As the light failed, his neighbour lit a lamp, and Zo could see the shadow of the aqueduct man moving about in his bedroom, then coming to stand by the courtyard door, probably looking out like Zo was doing. Zo's own room was dark; the aqueduct man would not have known he was there. The wind moved in the trees on the clifftop above them, and the scent of rosemary filled the air.

The sun went down, and Ahmos came to get Zo.

"Chrestos sent me," he said. "Always happy to help."

"I know," said Zo, trying to be gracious about it. Some nights it was easier than others.

He brought his flute, just in case, and sure enough, Mistress Aula said she wanted him to play for the dignitary and his party. So at least he didn't have to send somebody back for it. But having to be out in the front of the house without his crutch, on a day when he truly couldn't walk without it, put him in a foul mood.

The dignitary turned out to be one of those tedious foreigners who didn't understand how the tea houses of Tykanos worked. Usually they would think either that they were at a private party and didn't have to pay, or that they were in a brothel. This one did both. He had been brought by the purser from the fort, and at first seemed to think the Red Balconies was the purser's house. When he realized his mistake, he laughed uproariously—the purser was less amused—said, "Oh, *companions*, eh?" with a leer, and began doing a child's counting-off rhyme between Menthe and Pani.

"Both my lovely girls will be happy to entertain you," Mistress Aula purred. The dignitary's eyes bulged, and she added quickly, "here in our charming gathering. And perhaps later, if you desire a tête-à-tête with *one* of them, you may speak to me."

Menthe and Pani were indentured to the house, so if Mistress asked a favour, they wouldn't have much choice, and the dignitary might yet get what he wanted. But he looked confused, and Theano, who was mistress of ceremonies for the evening, caught Zo's eye and wiggled her fingers in a "play your flute" gesture. He picked up his instrument and put it to his lips.

That was when he noticed that the aqueduct man had joined them. He was leaning over awkwardly to talk to Taris, offering her something. Money, Zo realized. He was asking her, "Where do I pay?" She pointed toward the attendant guarding the incense burner, then got up to walk over with him, as if she thought he might lose his way.

As Zo played, he watched them return to their seats, the aqueduct man folding himself down onto a cushion beside Taris, his expression tense. He was a tall, rangy man, perhaps twenty years older than Zo, with a lean, strong-boned face. In daylight there was a weathered look to him, his skin freckled by the sun, his short, loosely curly hair a faded red. His eyes were a blue so light that they looked faded too. In the lamplit courtyard, he looked colourless, out of place.

When Zo played for an audience at the tea house, it always interested him to watch for the people who were really listening, who ignored their companions in favour of focussing on his music. His playing was worth listening to; he knew that. When he had spotted the people who were paying attention—if there were any—he liked to play for them, ignoring everyone else.

That evening, the guest of honour listened for a few moments before turning away—actually physically turning away—to flirt with Menthe and Pani at the same time, while Mistress Aula tried to adjudicate. The purser who had brought him was chatting with the third member of their party, another military type, and Taris and Theano each had guests of their own to entertain. Chrestos, bored with no one to talk to, looked like he had fallen asleep. The only one really listening to Zo was the aqueduct man.

Their eyes met, because he was not just listening, he was watching Zo's performance as if it was the only reason to be there, a politeness not usually extended to performers in the tea houses. His mouth quirked into a brief smile as he saw Zo looking at him, and Zo wondered what kind of smile to call it. Not a flirtatious smile, not even simply an appreciative smile. An *encouraging* smile, as if to assure Zo that he was enjoying the performance. How strangely charming.

"Sorry to abandon you like that," said Taris, shifting over to sit next to Hylas again.

"What? No, I ... "

He could not ask her to go on ignoring him so that he could listen to the music. But he did not understand how everyone else could be talking instead of paying attention to the performance. It was such lovely music. Hylas didn't know much about music, but he knew when something moved him, and Zo's flute-playing seemed to go straight into his heart and curl up there.

But Taris seemed to notice, without being told, that he was enraptured by the music, and she did not pursue the conversation until Zo was finished playing.

"I'm so glad you decided to join us tonight," she said then. "We've all been wondering whether you ever would."

"Oh, I—I—" They'd *all* been wondering? That meant they had been talking about him together, which was terrifying. "I happened to be free tonight ... "

"And how do we compare to the other houses?" She gave him what he thought was a rather mischievous smile. Ah, it was because she was letting him know that *she* knew that he'd been to the other houses.

"How—how did you know I've been to the other houses?" he asked, feeling pleased that he had been able to enter into the spirit of her joke.

Taris laughed. "Where else could you have been? You always come in late, and I don't think you're out until all hours working at the government office. I know they close up early."

"You are very p-perceptive. It is true. I do go to the other houses. But ... that is only because Governor Loukianos seems to like me to come with him. Perhaps he feels he has a host's duty, because he brought me to the island."

39

"You wouldn't have gone otherwise?" Taris gave him an arch look. "When the tea houses are Tykanos's pride and joy?"

"Well, I … I hate to make the companions put up with me."

"Why, what do you do?"

"Nothing, nothing." He was aghast before realizing that he was being teased again. "Er. I sit there stupidly."

She shrugged. "There's no shame in that, if it's what you feel like doing. We're here to provide entertainment, not the other way around. But it seems to me you're not enjoying yourself at the other houses, and *that's* why you wouldn't go, if the governor weren't dragging you with him."

Hylas laughed. "Yes, you're quite right. I—I didn't mean to blame the companions, that's all. It's my fault for not being able to appreciate what they offer. Not their fault, not in the least."

Taris looked like she wanted to argue, perhaps out of professional pride—no, we ought to be able to make you enjoy yourself, if we're good at our job—and honestly, Hylas could understand that. He'd have had the same impulse if they had been talking about, say, the construction of a bridge. Perhaps that wasn't an exact analogy.

"Well, but you haven't answered my first question," she said. "How *do* we compare to the other houses?"

He didn't want to insult her or the Red Balconies, but he also didn't want to lie.

"It feels … more homey here," he said. "Though perhaps that is because I live here."

She smiled a little wryly. "Perhaps."

"The music exceeds anything I have heard elsewhere," he offered, and it was quite true.

"Zo's awfully good, isn't he? But his health is poor, unfortunately, and he doesn't always have the strength to play."

"Oh," said Hylas, and didn't know what else to say. It was

devastating to think that the performance he'd enjoyed so much might have taken a toll on the performer. But also, for reasons he couldn't quite untangle, the prospect of talking about Zo made him nervous.

The other male companion, Chrestos, came up then and draped himself across a couple of pillows on Hylas's opposite side.

"Don't monopolize the aqueduct man, Taris," he drawled. "After all, I'm the one who talked him into coming tonight."

"What, really? Is that true?"

"N-no, well, I guess he did give me the idea." Hylas felt his cheeks heating.

"You see," said Chrestos triumphantly.

"Well, whatever it was, I'm glad of it," said Taris. "Refill his cup, will you, Chrestos, like a good boy?"

Chrestos rolled his eyes and huffed, but he obeyed, which meant getting up from his languid pose to fetch a new pitcher of wine.

"Chrestos is usually busy with his patron, Captain Themistokles," Taris remarked when he was gone.

"Oh," said Hylas, again not sure how to respond.

Was he supposed to know the name Themistokles, or … No, he was being tactfully reminded that Chrestos was taken, had an exclusive patron, which was what the companions called their lovers. He hoped that was not because he'd been inappropriately friendly with Chrestos, given anyone the wrong idea …

"Ah, we're going to hear some more music," said Taris, pointing to where one of the other companions, a dark-haired woman whose name Hylas thought was Theano, was tuning a lyre. "You'll like to listen to this."

Hylas smiled gratefully. Chrestos returned to fill his cup with wine and lounge on the cushions again, and someone passed around a plate of delicate sesame cakes. No one tried to talk to Hylas while Theano played. He drank his wine and ate his cake and listened to the clear notes of the lyre and her rich voice singing songs from Pheme.

He glanced around for Zo, wondering whether he had retired after his own performance, but he was still there, sitting with a couple of newly arrived guests, deep in conversation.

The aqueduct man had arrived early, and he left early, retiring to his room after saying goodnight to Taris and Chrestos, as a new wave of late-night guests arrived in the courtyard. Zo envied him.

It was another hour before he was able to make his own escape, and then only because the guests he was sitting with insisted that he looked tired. He was tired, and his body ached all over. He had to wait for Ahmos to carry him back to his room, but because he was in ill spirits, and tired, and both of those things caused him to make poor decisions, he insisted on being set down at his door rather than carried inside.

Of course this meant that he stumbled making his way through his room in the dark and nearly knocked over the lamp stand. He caught the stand and righted it, but he heard the lamp smash on the floor.

He stood holding onto the cold metal shaft of the lamp stand, waiting for his eyes to adjust to the dark enough to see the pieces of the clay lamp and the puddle of oil on the floor. He could just pick his way around them and get to his bed. Perhaps he should do that. But the idea of waking tomorrow morning to see that mess on the floor made him want to cry.

He thought longingly of the time when he used to be able to summon a servant to deal with a situation like this— when he wouldn't even have needed to summon anyone, because someone would have been there already, because he would never have been blundering about in a dark room by himself. Now he was actually beginning to cry, tears trickling helplessly out of his eyes.

He drew a deep breath and told himself to be calm. What could he do in this moment? The nearest light was all the way back in the courtyard. He could go back to the door and look out and see if Ahmos was still within hailing distance. Or ... there it was, beyond the garden door, the glow of lamplight from his neighbour's room.

He went to his desk and peered into his hand mirror in the dark to make sure the tears hadn't tracked his eye makeup down his face in a shocking way. As far as he could tell, they hadn't. He took a taper from the drawer where he kept them, patted his way along the wall until he found his crutch, and went out into the garden.

The lattice door to Hylas's room had been slid half open. Zo made a fist and knocked on the lattice, making an unassertive, rattling sound, but loud enough in the quiet at the back of the house. Hylas was sitting on his bed, crossed-legged, and he started at the sound.

"Come in?" he said uncertainly.

He got down from the bed, and when Zo stepped into the open doorway, he was standing, with the look of a man half-prepared for attack, tall and rather daunting in the lamplight.

"Hello," he said. "Ah, you've got a cane! Or more of a ... crutch sort of thing. I am so glad. I—I mean, because that means you can get around by yourself."

"Yes," said Zo, "barely."

"It's just that I'd never ... I wasn't sure ... Is there anything ... "

"May I get a light?" Zo held up the taper indicatively. "It's dark in my room, and I ... dropped something."

"Of course!"

Hylas sprang toward the lamp on its stand beside his bed,

43

the twin of the one in Zo's own room. Apparently Pantaleon hadn't made off with that when he took the rest of the furniture. The aqueduct man unhooked the lamp from its chain and brought it over to the door. Zo put his taper to the flame and waited for it to catch.

"Thank you," he said. "Did you enjoy this evening's entertainment?"

Hylas looked up from the lamp flame, and their eyes met. "I enjoyed your playing, very much."

Zo smiled. "Thank you for listening so attentively."

The taper had caught and burned brightly. Zo withdrew it from the lamp flame.

"It was my pleasure," said Hylas.

Zo carried the burning taper back to his room, lit a candle on his desk, and cleaned up the broken lamp on the floor. By the time he shed his outer clothes, blew out the candle, and crawled into bed, the light from next door had gone out too, so presumably the aqueduct man had also gone to bed.

CHAPTER 5

HYLAS CARRIED his breakfast tray out into the back courtyard as usual, then hesitated. He knew that Zo was up; he'd glimpsed him, on the way to the kitchen, going into the privy. That didn't mean he wanted company.

Finally Hylas made up his mind and set the tray down on a rock near his own door. He went to Zo's door and knocked tentatively on the frame of the lattice.

"Yes?" came Zo's voice after a moment.

"I, um … "

"You can open it."

"Oh."

Hylas slid open the screen. Zo was sitting in a chair at what might have been either a desk or a dressing table— maybe both, as it had writing materials and makeup on it. His black hair was pulled back into a short, careless pigtail, and his eyes were not painted, which made him look freshly, differently beautiful.

"Good morning," Hylas said. "They always give me two cups with my tea and more buns than I can eat. Do you— would you—like to join me?"

"Thank you," said Zo, and Hylas was so sure it would be

the beginning of "Thank you, but no," that he was quite startled when Zo pushed back his chair from his desk.

"Oh, you—you will?"

The companion paused. "Did you not want me to say yes?"

"No! No, I … I did. I wasn't sure whether you usually breakfast at this hour." That made some sense; he felt proud of himself.

Zo smiled. "Usually I'm trying to fall back to sleep at this hour. But not today, so I'd be happy to join you."

He rose from his desk with difficulty and leaned on his crutch as he came out into the garden. The crutch was just a long staff with a small cross-piece at the top, surely not the best design for its purpose. Hylas ran to pick up the tray from where he had left it and carried it over to the chair near Zo's door.

"You can bring out one of the chairs from my room for yourself," Zo suggested.

Hylas considered that for a moment. "But we don't have a table," he said. "So we'd have nowhere to put the tea things … I'll just sit on the ground and hand things to you. That'll work better."

Zo was giving him a doubtful look. In the sunlight and without his makeup, he looked strikingly young. Hylas was seized with a feeling of shame that he had for so long ignored someone who might have benefited from his help and company, simply because he'd found Zo's beauty intimidating.

"You probably find it easier to get up from a chair than from a cushion on the ground," Hylas went on, not sure how else to show consideration than by baldly spelling it out. "I understand. Sitting cross-legged is hard on one's knees. We don't do it so much where I'm from."

Zo moved finally to sit in his chair, giving Hylas a wry smile. "Don't you mostly recline on couches?"

"Where I'm actually from, no—we usually sat on stools and benches and things."

He sat down on the grass beside Zo's chair, putting down the tea tray, and for the first time he filled both of the bowls on the tray with tea. He lifted one carefully, holding it with both hands, to offer it to Zo, and their eyes met, as they had the night before over the lamp flame. And again, there seemed to be something there, a connection warm as the steam rising from the tea, bright as the light from the lamp flame. Though perhaps it was only how a well-trained companion looked at anyone. Whatever it was, Hylas appreciated it.

Zo blew on the surface of his tea, the bowl poised in his long, elegant fingers. He sipped it. Hylas tried not to stare at his mouth. He was so young, and so tired; it seemed like taking advantage.

"Mm. This is the good tea for guests. They must like you in the kitchen."

"Oh. They may. I like them. We have good chats when I go there." He realized that must sound implausible, that he could actually have a satisfactory conversation with anyone. But the kitchen staff were very talkative.

"Last night … " Zo began delicately. When he hesitated, it sounded artful, not as if he was searching desperately for the right word or wondering if he should say this at all. "You said you were glad I can get around by myself with my crutch. That was kind of you."

"Oh!" It had burst out of him, and he'd been quite sure it had been inappropriate and unwelcome. He thought he'd even seen Zo's beautiful eyebrows contract in a frown. "Well, I—I meant it."

"Yes." Zo gave him a sidelong look, elegantly unreadable. "You strike me as a man who is not in the habit of saying things he does not mean."

That made Hylas laugh. "I—I say things I don't mean all the time. But only without meaning to. If, uh, if you follow."

"I believe I do."

After a moment's silence, during which they sipped their tea, Hylas tried to say something that he'd been struggling to put into words. "You—you don't have to be charming, when it's just me."

Zo gave him a wide-eyed look. "You think I can help it?"

Then they were both laughing. Zo had a beautiful, dark laugh, surprisingly rich and totally infectious.

"Actually," he said, sobering but still smiling, "I appreciate the sentiment."

"Oh, that's ... well. Good." Hylas picked up the basket of buns and offered it. "There's different kinds. I think the ones with sesame seeds are sweet. Oh, you probably know that."

"I like the salty ones," said Zo, picking out a bun. "Thanks."

They sat in silence for a time after that, drinking their tea and eating buns. They could hear birds crying overhead on the cliff face, and a breeze moved through the garden, circulating the scent of rosemary.

"I love this garden," Hylas remarked, almost to himself.

"Thank you. It's not at its best right now."

He looked at Zo, surprised. "It's yours? I mean—you planted it?"

Zo nodded. "Some of it. I designed it all, and I take care of it when I can. I'm not always an invalid, and I'm not in a permanent decline—it comes and goes. Some days I'm able to work in my garden."

"Ah, truly? That is wonderful."

"Milo, the bouncer here before Ahmos, used to help me. He's the one who started building the terraces back there. But he earned his freedom and went home to Pyria a few months ago."

"I'll help you." The words were out of Hylas's mouth

before he could consider their wisdom. He rephrased: "Could I help you? I don't know anything about gardening, but—well, I don't know much, but I've been learning a few things lately. Governor Loukianos is always talking to me about his garden."

"I've heard the governor's garden is magnificent. I've always wanted to see it."

"I like yours better," said Hylas truthfully.

"But you just said you don't know anything about gardens."

"That's true, I did."

"I'll teach you what I know, and then you'll understand that the governor's is much more impressive than mine."

"Does that mean that I can help maintain it for you?"

"Of course. I'd be very grateful."

And yet there was a whole houseful of people he might have asked, if he had wanted to. Was it absurd of Hylas to feel honoured that he was allowed to help?

"I do know how to build walls," he said. Better than this Milo, he didn't add.

"I suppose you would."

They sat and ate buns and sipped tea in silence for a few minutes. The time stretched out without feeling awkward, more like being quiet with an old friend than with a stranger. Not that Zo could have qualified as an "old" friend to anyone Hylas's age. In a different life, Hylas might have had a son or daughter who could have been Zo's contemporary.

"Do you get out into the town much?" Hylas asked. "When you're, when you're feeling up to it?"

Zo shook his head. "It's troublesome to go out, so I generally don't. Mind you, the girls don't go out much either. We're not really supposed to be available to meet in the streets, you know? You have to come to one of the houses to see us. We can't be too free with our company."

"I suppose that makes sense," Hylas allowed.

"And I'm not supposed to walk around much, even in the house."

"Not supposed to—you mean your physician has told you not to?" Hylas asked with concern.

Zo gave a short laugh. "No, Mistress Aula has told me not to. 'It's all very well to pretend to be ill, but you've got to do it prettily.' Which means lying in bed or letting myself be carried if I insist on going anywhere."

"Is that—is that what you quarrelled about?" Hylas blurted, remembering what Taris had told him in that outpouring of unsolicited gossip a few days ago. He should have phrased it differently; Zo would wonder how he knew they had quarrelled.

But Zo simply nodded. "I gave in, in the end. I don't go out or insist on hobbling around with my crutch. I let Ahmos carry me." He shrugged. "It is easier that way."

"I don't think you like it, though," Hylas guessed. "You'd prefer to do things for yourself when you can. As anyone would."

Zo looked at him. "Do you think so? I sometimes feel it's unduly troublesome of me."

"I think … " Hylas spoke slowly, choosing his words with care. "I think it is good to be able to accept help when you need it. Not everyone can. But when you don't need it—it's not troublesome to want to do things for yourself. Especially things that other people take for granted."

"Mm. Perhaps you're right. Is there more tea?"

"Oh—yes. I beg your pardon, I should notice when your cup is empty and fill it, shouldn't I? As I'm, er, sort of the host here."

Zo laughed. "It's all right. If I don't have to be charming, I can just *ask* for more tea."

Hylas refilled his bowl and passed it up to him.

"So tell me what else needs to be done in the garden, besides finishing that wall."

"Did you know he's a hero?" Pani said at lunch.

"Who?" asked Zo.

"He saved a whole village from a flood," said Menthe.

"Koilas, on Pheme," said Chrestos, who was fastidiously picking individual seeds out of a halved pomegranate. "It's a town, not a village."

"Who?" Zo repeated.

"It's a village," said Menthe.

"The aqueduct man," said Pani to Zo finally. "What's his name?"

"Hylas. How did he save a village?" Zo demanded. Images of that soft-spoken man standing alone against an invading army or running with armloads of children ahead of a roaring fire jostled absurdly in his mind.

"With engineering," said Taris.

"Oh." That made more sense.

"They were damming a river down from the mountain," said Pani, picking up the story, "and there was a fatal flaw in the construction—"

"It would have flooded the whole town—"

"Village."

"It would have flooded the whole *valley*, only he caught it in time."

"Wasn't it his job to catch it, if he's an engineer?" Theano spoke for the first time. She was older than the other companions, and the one who usually said things like this.

"Yes," said Pani, "but he wasn't the engineer in charge of the dam, you see, he was just an underling, and at first the chief engineer wouldn't listen to him, and he had to go over his head, which got him in trouble—only in the end, they all saw he was right and had saved the village. Town, whatever. A bunch of people who lived in that valley."

"He became quite famous for it, apparently. They gave him an official commendation in Pheme."

"If I weren't so busy, I'd cultivate him," said Chrestos. "But Captain Themistokles takes up *all* my time."

"The tenants aren't here to be 'cultivated,' Chrestos," said Theano. "They're here to pay rent."

"It's true," said Menthe. "What if you got involved with him and then wanted to break it off, but he was *living here*? Ugh."

It was a good point. You wouldn't want to try to negotiate an affair with someone who was living in the same house. The potential for awkwardness was too great.

Not that Zo had been having much luck getting a lover from *outside* the house, either. He'd had hopes of Djosi, who was perhaps not as much of a prize as Chrestos's never-ending Captain Themistokles, but was personally much more interesting and to Zo's eye better-looking. He'd even thought their first night together had gone reasonably well—as well as these things usually went, with a minimum of awkwardness. But then Djosi hadn't been back, hadn't written a note or sent a gift or anything, and it didn't look good.

"It's nice to have you join us, Zo," said Menthe tentatively. "It seems … it's been a while since you've eaten lunch with us instead of in your room."

"I suppose so," said Zo.

He wasn't sure why he had felt like coming out to join them today. Perhaps it was having breakfasted with someone —a totally novel experience—that had made him want company now.

Hylas sat at the desk that he had politely commandeered in the corner of the Tykanos government office, sketching on a fresh leaf of his tablet. He was at loose ends.

He'd borrowed several idle men from the government office and done a rough-and-ready survey of the spring on the little island. He'd written a report about it which he did not think the governor had read. He had finished a preliminary assessment of the town's water supply, identifying several places where he suspected broken pipes, but no one could tell him who was in charge of digging them up to find out. He'd visited the bath house near the Red Balconies that was always closed, and after asking several people found out that the reason was something to do with the water intake, which kept filling up with sand and having to be laboriously dredged. No one knew who was supposed to fix that, either. Mutari, the quartermaster's mistress and key to assembling a proper survey team, was due back from Gylphos with the next supply ship, tomorrow or the next day. It didn't seem worth coming up with another project to occupy himself for so short a time. Perhaps he should go fishing, he thought, or sea-bathing, or …

He'd delayed too long, because Loukianos had come into the office—he could hear the governor's voice in the anteroom—and that meant that once his state of idleness was discovered, he'd be invited out to a tea house. Poetry would be recited. Women would try gamely to flirt with him. Could he invite the governor out fishing instead?

"There you are, Hylas!" came the inevitable greeting. Loukianos wove through the desks to lean over Hylas's. "What are you drawing there?"

Hylas looked down at the tablet, which he'd forgotten was open. He'd been sketching a plan for completing the terraces in Zo's garden. "Oh, just something I'm building. In my spare time," he added hastily, though why he still had that instinct with Loukianos, given the man's approach to leisure, was beyond him.

"Good, good! Let me know if you need anything. I take it you're not busy this afternoon?"

"No, I am not. I was thinking of taking a walk down to the beach."

"Ah. That's an idea. I haven't visited the beach lately. I used to go pretty frequently at one time." Loukianos looked almost perplexed for a moment, as if he'd forgotten why he used to go, or why he had stopped. "Yes, I know a good place," he went on, warming to the idea. "The Eastern Beach. I could take you there if you like."

Hylas would have been happy to go by himself, but he wasn't craving solitude, and so long as they didn't end up back at the Bower of Suos or—worse—the Amber Lily, he would be happy to have Loukianos's company.

And he was. They walked down through the town, past the fort on a footpath that led to a sheltered, sandy beach. They strolled in the sun and bathed in the sea, then sat on a rock to dry off, and Loukianos told stories about his time in Sasia. It was a good afternoon.

"I haven't done this in far too long," Loukianos remarked as they dressed on the shore. "I used to come here pretty often with … Well. Once upon a time."

It had occurred to Hylas to wonder if Loukianos was mourning someone. He often seemed like a man filling time that had maybe in the past been taken up by the presence of someone else. There was no wife in the governor's mansion, that Hylas had noticed. Maybe he was a widower.

It would have been a reasonable moment for Hylas to confess that he enjoyed the beach more than the tea houses. He could have phrased it tactfully and probably avoided offending. He was used enough to Loukianos by now that he thought he could have managed that. But he decided it would be kinder to say nothing about that. Maybe part of his job here *was* to be the governor's friend, after all.

"Thank you for accompanying me," he said instead. "I've enjoyed myself."

CHAPTER 6

THE NEXT MORNING when Hylas came out of his room with his tray, Zo was already up and sitting on his chair in the garden. He had combed his hair and left it loose, and he was wrapped in a shawl against the cool morning air.

Hylas smiled when he saw him, an unmistakable expression of relief in his eyes. Zo had thought Hylas meant to knock on his door again and might be glad to be spared from actually having to do it.

"I hoped I was in time to join you for tea again," Zo said.

"Absolutely."

Hylas put down his tray and sat on the cushion by Zo's chair as he had done the day before. He'd thrown a shawl of his own over his arm, and took a moment to unfold it and sling it around his shoulders before pouring the tea. It was a surprisingly bright green, striking with his reddish hair.

"I got this in town on Market Day," he said, touching the fabric, perhaps having noticed Zo looking at it. "I thought I might like to have a few nice things." He spoke as if it was a novel idea.

He passed a bowl of tea up to Zo, the steam curling in the crisp, early light.

"It's beautiful," Zo said, cradling the warm bowl. "The colour suits you."

Hylas looked as if that completely flummoxed, even alarmed him.

"It's very satisfying to have nice things," Zo went on quickly. "You can get a lot of good quality in the market here. Even though Tykanos is such a small place. And there's food from all over, too. Have you tried any of the Glifian specialties yet?"

Hylas finished one of the buns in a couple of bites. He shook his head. "Not really. We keep going to the Amber Lily, where they hardly serve any food at all, and the Bower of Suos has very Pseuchaian dishes. A lot of fish."

"Ah, so those are the houses the governor favours? He's never come here, since I've been here. Although I've heard that he used to, years ago."

"Well, he will be back, I guess, because he has promised to take me to all the tea houses on the island."

"Are you eager to go?" Zo asked doubtfully.

Hylas looked up at him with a wry smile. "No, I'd be happy to stay home. Even if my home weren't also a tea house—and a better one."

Zo let out an uncalculated laugh. "We're better than the Amber Lily?"

"Immortal gods, *I* think so. It's the dullest place." He stopped, pressing his lips together, as if he feared he had said too much. "I—I mean … "

"Are you worried I might have friends there?" Zo guessed.

"Yes. That is exactly what I … "

"I don't. I don't know anyone at the other tea houses. I've never even been in any of them, except once to a party at Myrrha's, a long time ago. I came to the Red Balconies when I arrived on Tykanos, and I've stayed here ever since—and you already know I don't go out much."

"Ah. Then you don't know how boring the Amber Lily is."

Zo snickered. "It's generally ranked first among the Jewels of Tykanos. Agathe and Zenais are supposed to be the most beautiful women between Glif and Pheme."

"Oh. Well, that's not my … I mean, I don't really … " A blush spread over Hylas's cheekbones.

"No, me neither," Zo said quickly, surprised to find the topic so awkward. "So—I didn't realize you were famous."

"What? I'm not."

"Apparently you are, though. You saved a village outside Pheme from flooding due to a faulty dam?"

Hylas gulped his tea. "Oh, that. I may have done. I mean, it might have flooded, if I hadn't done anything—or it might not. It was the type of cement we were using. I didn't think—don't think—it would have held up under the proposed design." He refilled his bowl. "I just happened to have experience using the same formulation on a couple of bridges, and I'd seen what it could and could not withstand. The chief engineer was concerned to save face, which unfortunately caused the situation to escalate, and the whole thing was … talked about."

"You stood up to him," Zo translated, "and he tried to brazen it out, even though he knew you were right—and you ended up with a commendation from the archons, so someone must have agreed with you."

Hylas nodded. "I went over his head, consulted an architect in Pheme—the thing ended up in court. It was insubordinate, but … well, we weren't in the army."

"You risked your career. It was courageous of you."

Hylas laughed awkwardly. "No, I … don't think it was anything like that."

"Was it a long time ago? When you were young?"

"It was three years ago. I was … not young. Thirty-seven.

But I was still a junior engineer on the project. I'm good at my job, but I haven't been doing it very long."

That was intriguing. "What did you do before?"

"Well. I was born and raised in Ariata." He looked at Zo, maybe expecting a reaction. "Do you know much about Ariata?"

"Er … no." He settled for that. All he really knew about Ariata was that certain people from his childhood had always been concerned about going to war with it. It had, at the time, seemed like an unimaginably faraway place.

Hylas said, "In Ariata, families of my parents' class give their sons to the state to be raised in the barracks. So I was brought up to be a soldier."

"How cruel! Do you mean to say that the nobles make them give up their children?"

"Ah. No, we *were* the nobles. It's what the aristocratic families do. The peasants aren't allowed that honour."

"The honour of sacrificing their sons to the state? Holy God."

"Well … yes."

"So you were a soldier then, before you became an engineer." It didn't fit at all, and Zo wasn't sure he believed it.

"No. No, I was never a soldier. I didn't complete my training." He took another swallow of tea. "It is a long story."

And it didn't seem to be one he wanted to tell—or perhaps it was that he didn't think Zo would want to hear it.

"Do you ever go down to the Eastern Beach?" Hylas asked abruptly. "No—you told me that you don't go out much, so that is probably a foolish question. It's just that I was there yesterday, and I thought you might like it."

"I don't think I've ever been," said Zo truthfully.

"I think you might like it. I already said that. You could float in the water, I thought, which you might find relaxing, and nobody much seems to go there, so you wouldn't have to worry about being too much in public."

"It sounds lovely," said Zo.

He waited for the invitation that this had surely been leading up to, wondering what he should say. Probably just that he didn't feel up to it—that would be simple enough.

There was a long silence. Finally Zo realized that no invitation was coming. Perhaps Hylas imagined him going to the beach with someone else, a patron or one of the other companions. Perhaps he didn't know how to ask.

Perhaps he thought he'd have to pay for incense to take Zo to the beach, and he didn't want to.

Hylas walked up the steep streets to the governor's mansion, feeling an odd sense of dissatisfaction. He'd wanted to invite Zo to the beach. It should have been so simple. Hylas was the one who had been to the beach and knew where it was; he could arrange everything, hire a chair and bearers for Zo and bring blankets and everything that he would need to be comfortable.

But it wasn't simple. He'd learned already, in the time he'd spent at the tea houses with the governor and his friends, that the companions enjoyed varying degrees of freedom. Some could come and go more or less as they liked, others were bound by contracts that restricted who they could see and what they could do outside their houses, and some were essentially slaves, indentured to the landlords who owned the houses. He didn't know which Zo was, and he could not begin to think how to ask.

He arrived at the governor's mansion and was shown through to Loukianos's garden. Another place he would have liked to bring Zo, if such a thing were possible. But perhaps Loukianos himself would know how to make the invitation. That was a thought.

Loukianos was leaning on the stone railing of one of his

garden's terraces, next to a tall, copper-skinned woman dressed in the type of pleated white gown that Hylas had learned was fashionable in Gylphos—Glif, as the locals called it.

"Hylas, here you are!" the governor exclaimed. "This is Mutari from the House of the Peacock. Hylas here is the engineer I've been telling you about."

The tall woman gave Hylas a gracious smile. He thought he could have guessed from that smile that she was a companion, even if Loukianos hadn't mentioned her house. He smiled back.

"I hear you need some surveying done, Hylas," she said.

"That's right."

"Which island are we talking about? The big or the little?"

"The big island," said Hylas.

"The little island," said Loukianos at the same time. "Oh. Er. I think you mean the little island, don't you?"

Hylas shook his head. As he'd assumed, Loukianos had not read his report. "I've been to the spring on the little island. The water quality isn't good—probably something to do with the soil that it travels through—and I'm afraid the spring is too sluggish to provide enough volume even for a bath house or anything of that kind. I haven't been able to get to the big island myself yet, but I've been told by several people that the water there is of a much better quality."

"Hm," said Loukianos, frowning.

"You know what the problems are with building on the big island, don't you?" said Mutari.

"I … am afraid I … "

"No, no, he doesn't," Loukianos interrupted. "By the gods, I was hoping it wouldn't come to this. You're sure that water is bad, Hylas?"

"I'm afraid everyone I took with me to the site agreed, sir

—it has a bitter taste. It might not be unwholesome, but people wouldn't want to drink it."

"Or make tea with it," Mutari supplied.

"Exactly."

"All right, all right. Let's sit down, all of us, and have a talk."

He pushed off the railing and led the way toward a grotto with benches at the opposite end of the terrace. Hylas and Mutari followed him.

"We do need a new aqueduct badly," Mutari remarked.

"I know," said Hylas. "I've just finished an assessment of the water supply in town, and it's not adequate. I think repairs need to be undertaken, and I suspect some house-holders may have tapped into the pipes to divert water to their own property."

"Oh, they all do that up here," said Loukianos gloomily. "All the merchants who live up here on the mountain. There's some old law that they claim means I can't stop them or tax them for it or anything. Drives me wild, honestly."

Mutari reached across and touched Hylas's shoulder lightly. "We'll figure something out."

"Right," said Loukianos, when they were seated in the grotto. "You know the history, I daresay. The small island of Tykanos used to belong to Boukos, and the Boukossians still govern the villages on the North coast—which is an adminis-trative goat-fuck, but that's another story. In any case, when Boukos agreed to let Pheme build the naval base here, they ceded control of the town, which is when Pheme first installed a governor."

"If I may, Loukianos," Mutari interrupted gracefully. "The salient point is that the big island never belonged to Boukos *or* Pheme."

"Exactly," said Loukianos. "Thank you, my dear. I was wandering from the point. The big island, Hylas, with all the timber but no decent harbour, has always been claimed by Gylphos."

That is, it belonged to the mainland kingdom off whose coast the islands were situated.

"Ah," said Hylas. "I didn't realize."

He also didn't entirely understand why this was a problem. Relations between Gylphos and the Pseuchaian League were good, he'd thought. At least they were at peace and traded in grain and dates and flax and things. Certainly the island of Tykanos itself was full of Gylphians coming and going. Mutari was surely Gylphian herself.

"It's caused tension, of course," Loukianos went on, "the islands being divided like that. Obviously Pheme would like to be able to log the big island, and the Gylphians would like to have control of a good harbour. But the compromise used to work—they sold us timber cheaply, and we let them use the harbour with only token tariffs. Waived altogether in far too many cases if you ask me, but just *try* getting that changed."

"The problem is," Mutari cut in delicately again, "that Glif—Gylphos—has come under the control of the Sasian throne. It was not a bloody conquest, and our queen is still on her throne, but she answers to the king in Suna now."

"That means … " Hylas started. "What does that mean? That if we want to build on the big island, we'll have to ask permission from … Sasia?"

He'd thought the obstacles to building this aqueduct consisted of some jurisdictional pettiness and maybe some engineering difficulties, but apparently they had to contend with the might of the kingdom of Sasia—Zash, to give it its proper name—ancient and implacable enemy of all Pseuchaia. This was beginning to become nightmarish.

"Not Sasia exactly," Mutari clarified. "Just the Gylphian officials who may or may not be Sasian puppets at this point."

"It's hard to say what's going on over there," said Loukianos. "But it's not impossible. We might be able to do it."

"I must also warn you," said Mutari, "you're not proposing simply to build on the island—you want to take fresh water from it. My people and the Sasians are both very, mm, protective of water sources. There are various religious prohibitions and legal penalties … " She smiled apologetically.

"I understand," said Hylas. "What do you recommend we do?"

"Let me speak to Phileidion," she said. "The quartermaster at the fort, my patron. I'll explain to him what you need. The first thing is to get the survey done. After that … I'll see what I can do."

Hylas hoped that didn't mean she was going to have to seduce someone. He wondered if there was any way to tell her so and concluded there probably wasn't.

Mornings at the Red Balconies were spent doing chores. The house was short on servants, so there was work for everyone. That morning, because it was still cold, they had opened up the winter sitting room, and Menthe and Pani had brought their spinning to the divan under the sunlit windows. Zo had a basket of wool to card, and Leta, Theano's baby, was crawling on the floor, exploring the pattern of the rug and trying to snack on the tassels of the cushions.

A long, drawn-out wail came from somewhere near the front of the house. Menthe, Pani, and Zo exchanged startled glances, frozen with their work in their hands. For a moment, Zo expected the cry to be followed by the ritual wails of a Zashian house in mourning—it had been that kind of sound. But of course they were not in Zash. He could hear someone shouting furiously, and a lower voice replying. The baby giggled obliviously.

"Is that Mistress Aula?" asked Menthe.

"It sounds like her," Zo agreed.

They all exchanged glances again, then looked back down at their work, no one making a move to rise. The mistress's bad tempers were a danger to everyone; she had a tendency to lash out indiscriminately, and they had all learned the hard way to avoid her when she was in a rage about something.

Of course you couldn't avoid any situation for very long in a house the size of the Red Balconies. Only a few minutes had passed by the time Theano opened the door of the winter sitting room and slipped inside.

"I thought you'd all be hiding in here," she said drily. "Even Zo. Hello, Zo. But not Chrestos—where's he?"

"I'm not sure," said Zo. "Out with Captain Themistokles?"

"Mm. When in doubt." Theano scooped up Leta on her way across the room, and sat down under the window, where she bounced the baby absently.

"What's going on out there?" Menthe demanded. "Don't keep us in suspense."

"I thought you might like a few more peaceful moments of not knowing, but … " Theano shrugged. The baby had begun to make grabbing gestures toward her breasts, and she unpinned one shoulder of her gown. "The landlord has died."

"Is that all?" said Pani.

"We've been expecting that for months," said Menthe.

"Poor old man," Pani added.

So it had been a death, after all; Zo hadn't been imagining things when he thought of mourning wails. He didn't think there had been much real affection between Mistress Aula and the landlord. But you never knew.

"Sometimes you don't know how you'll react until it

actually happens," he said, unconvincingly even to himself. "Perhaps she is truly sad."

Menthe and Pani gave him pitying, aren't-you-sweet looks.

"She's angry," Theano said, looking down at the baby sucking quietly in her arms. "'Angry' isn't even the word. She's livid. He's left the Red Balconies to her."

"Holy God," Zo breathed.

"Orante's balls," said Pani.

CHAPTER 7

"It was nice to see you at our gathering last night," Zo said, as he and Hylas sat at breakfast in the garden the following morning.

"I'm glad I stayed home again," said Hylas. Gathering courage, he added, "I loved listening to you sing."

Zo looked slightly surprised, one of the fleeting expressions that never crossed his face when he was entertaining. "Thank you. I'd sing more often, but … I've been told my voice doesn't suit the tea house repertoire."

"Oh," said Hylas hopelessly. That was a level of analysis that was beyond him. He'd thought he was doing quite well to identify that Zo's voice reminded him of red wine: dark and rich.

"They're mostly songs written by women, about loving men." Zo had obviously been able to tell that he was confused. "And I have too deep a voice. I've been told it sounds 'lewd.'"

"That sounds … " Hylas cast about for a polite word. "Hypocritical?"

Zo laughed. "Probably. But Mistress Aula seems to agree, and she is in charge."

"She wasn't there last night," Hylas recalled.

"She's in mourning. The landlord died."

"Oh no. I'm sorry."

"He was old, and ill for a long time. It was expected. And no one liked him very much. Not even Mistress. If she had, perhaps she'd have put the whole house in mourning and closed for the day—I think that would be traditional." Zo shrugged. "But we can't exactly afford that."

"Still, she's mourning personally … "

"The landlord was her patron, ten years ago or more, when she was a companion at the Peacock."

"Oh, I didn't know."

"He bought the Red Balconies when it was in danger of being shut down—a couple of years before I came—and set her up as mistress. He's left it to her in his will. She's the landlady now."

"That's … That must be … " Hylas couldn't think what to say. It didn't sound good.

Zo spared him the trouble. "Nobody's happy about it. Especially not her. Apparently she was expecting a gift of money, or a property where she could retire and live in luxury, and the Red Balconies is very much not that."

"Oh dear. She couldn't sell it?"

"Not for the kind of money she wants, evidently. I'm getting this all second-hand from Theano, who's the only one of the women she really talks to."

Hylas wondered fleetingly what an establishment like the Red Balconies would sell for. He'd been considering his own finances the night before, and it had left him feeling rather rich. But that was only when he thought in terms of how many nights of incense he could afford to burn; he didn't have buying-the-whole-house money. Which reminded him that he still needed to speak to Governor Loukianos about his salary. The month's end had come and gone without any sign of a second payment.

"Anyway," said Zo, waving a hand dismissively, "it's too early to say what it will mean for all of us companions. There's no sense worrying about it yet."

Hylas nodded. "That's wise."

"So how is the aqueduct coming?"

Hylas groaned. "Don't mention the aqueduct. No, I mean, of course you may mention it—naturally you want to know about it, as it's my whole reason for being here. It's just that I'm beginning to worry it's never going to be built. We're currently waiting on someone's mistress convincing the Gylphians, or maybe the Sasians, to let us take water from the big island."

Zo smiled wryly. "Sounds very Tykanos."

"So I'm learning. Anyway, it does mean I have time to work in your garden today, if you'd like me to press on with the wall."

"I'd love that. It's the perfect weather for it. Warm sun, cool breeze."

"Yes."

They drank tea in silence for a few minutes. Hylas found himself looking up at Zo, at the sharp line of his jaw, the way his long hair fell over his shoulder.

"You sing and you play the flute," Hylas said thoughtfully. "What other talents do you have that I don't know about yet?"

Zo shrugged. "Just making conversation, I suppose. Gardening. Making myself look pretty." He rearranged the folds of his robe and smiled sidelong down at Hylas. "Up until I was seventeen, I had the same kind of education as most of the tea-house women. You know, poetry and music and how to look good in clothes. Mind you, most of the girls know how to weave and spin and sew too—I wish I'd learned anything so useful. I wish I'd spent time learning something like that instead of horse-riding, which I was never good at. You're trying to picture me on a horse now."

"I'm—I'm succeeding. You would look very well on a horse. But I don't think you would be comfortable. It must be hard on the joints, even for a good rider."

"Well, I was never that. What we all feel the lack of here is new books. They're expensive and hard to get on the island. And then our guests talk about things we haven't read, and it makes us feel unsophisticated. There's some new thing in Pheme that everyone is reading now, apparently—*The Bronze Dolphin*—and none of us had heard of it, but it's supposed to be really good. Apparently they have a copy at the Amber Lily, but it's no good asking them to lend it to us because—I'm sorry, this is extremely boring."

"No! I was just thinking that the governor is always asking if I want anything from Pheme, and that I could ask for some books."

"You don't have to do that!" Zo looked almost alarmed.

"Oh, I—I know, I didn't think you were hinting that I should, or ... I just thought it might be an idea."

Zo relaxed in his seat. "Forgive me, Hylas. It's a wonderful idea, so thoughtful of you."

"I'll ask him for a couple of treatises for myself, too. I don't own a copy of Manolios's *Principles*, and I really should, if I'm to continue to be a famous engineer."

"That's the spirit!" Zo flashed him one of his most dazzling smiles, lips a little parted, head thrown back.

Hylas returned the smile. He felt privileged to see the moments when Zo turned on his charm, like the opening of a tap to let water flow. It didn't diminish the effect, somehow. How had he become so skilled at such a young age?

"How long since you were seventeen?" Hylas asked without stopping to think whether the question was polite or not.

"Let me see ... five years? I haven't observed my birthday since then."

"Five years ago was when I left Ariata. I—I was a little more than seventeen."

"What made you leave?"

"My mother died. My sister was married already, so I had no one depending on me. I was free to leave. Finally."

"From what you told me of Ariata, I can understand why you wanted to leave."

Hylas nodded. He recalled that he hadn't really told Zo much.

"I wasn't fit for the army—I never understood why. I was strong and healthy, my wits were sound—I should have been able to turn myself to the task, but somehow I never could. There was always something in me that rebelled against it. I always seemed to want the opposite of what I was supposed to. I wanted ... to be gentle. I wanted to touch not to wound but to caress." Without intending it, his voice had dropped to a whisper. This was so difficult to talk about, even now.

"I was a failure as a man. There were others like me, a few that I knew, who didn't survive—they died in training or ran away. I survived, but I gave up a lot to do it. I was eventually proscribed—stripped of my aristocratic status—for being unable to inflict a killing blow on a slave in a training exercise. Well. Refusing to do it, that might be another way of putting it. My father was dead by this time, which made me the head of the family, so my mother and sister also lost their status. I was able to work to support them—as a commoner, certain trades were open to me that had not been before. I trained as an engineer.

"Ariata doesn't do big engineering projects—mostly what I did was build bridges in the countryside, now and then some work on siege machinery for the army. I was able to find enough work to provide for my mother until she died. But she always felt her loss of status. In Ariata, you cannot help it. There are places you aren't allowed to go, clothes you can't wear, people who won't see you—in the street, they literally will not look at you, they certainly won't have you in their homes. We had a comfortable house, we had servants—you can't own slaves as a commoner, but we had money to pay free servants—and we always had plenty to eat. We had—we *could* have had friends of our own class, but my mother would never allow it. She held herself above all our neighbours, which made us unpopular. My sister had to elope in order to marry a blacksmith in the country, and my mother never saw her again.

"I left after my mother died. The day I buried her ashes, my sea chest was packed, and I left. That was five years ago. Sometimes I feel as if I'm five years old, as if I was born the day I left Ariata."

"I had no idea," said Zo, his voice subdued. "All those lost years."

"Lost is the right word. Sometimes I think about what I might have been able to do with my life if I'd left sooner—sometimes I blame myself for not having the strength to do it. Just telling my mother that we were leaving Ariata and then going. But she didn't want to leave—she'd never been anywhere else, any more than I had, and I didn't know, when I was young, how different the rest of Pseuchaia was. I spent so long living in the knowledge that I was defective, a failed man, and it wasn't until I was in my thirties that I began to realize it was my homeland that was abnormal—there's nothing very unusual about me." He looked up and shook himself. "I daresay that was a lot more than you expected to hear me talk."

"Yes," said Zo frankly. "And it's hard to hear. My heart breaks for you. But I am glad you felt able to tell me."

"You're actually quite easy to talk to, once one gets over the … being intimidated by you. Not that—I know you don't mean to be intimidating."

"Oh, sometimes I do." Zo laughed.

"I've never known a man remotely like you," Hylas said, and it was still less than what he meant.

"I'm not exactly typical of anything. I did also grow up in a place where men *tend* to be warriors and statesmen and things and not courtesans."

"I never said I thought you were typical."

Zo laughed. "No, you didn't, did you? Well. Thank you." He was looking at Hylas from under his dark lashes, and he had managed to unearth the compliment Hylas had been trying ineptly to offer him.

"I had a thought," Hylas said suddenly. "The crutch that you use—I had an idea of how it could be redesigned to help you walk better."

Zo's eyebrows went up. "Oh, this is your famous engineer aspect coming to the fore again, I see."

"No, it's just—well. Maybe. But if there were a strut lower down for you to hold with your right hand, that could take more of your weight as you step, you see, and then … "

They spent the morning working in the garden together. The sun was warm on Zo's back as he sat and pulled weeds from the low beds. Hylas, in a one-shouldered work tunic, hefted and stacked stones for the terrace, quietly redoing the work that Milo had done. Even Zo could tell he was doing a better job. Every so often, under the pretext of taking a break, Zo looked up at Hylas. He had freckles on his shoulders and hair on his chest, not faded like the hair of his head but curls of bright orange.

I've never kissed a red-haired man, Zo thought irrelevantly.

Hylas didn't think of him that way. Zo had gotten pretty good, after five years at the Red Balconies, at telling when a man was interested, and Hylas showed none of the signs. The other companions had commented on his awkwardness;

perhaps he was uncomfortable with the whole concept of companions. Some men were.

Mistress Aula came out into the garden from Zo's room, startling him and Hylas with her sudden appearance.

"Oh, hello, madam," said Hylas, straightening up and brushing a lock of hair off his forehead with his wrist.

"I did knock," Aula began tartly, "but there was no answer."

She was dressed in undyed wool for mourning, although she had still put up her hair and wore jewellery, which Zo didn't think Pseuchaians in mourning were supposed to do. At least he knew their men weren't supposed to shave.

"I'm sorry," he said, struggling up from his seat on the grass. "We didn't hear you."

"I am sorry for your loss," said Hylas, and to Zo it sounded genuine. Of course—he wouldn't have said it if it hadn't been.

Mistress Aula sniffed. "I suppose you've heard that I am your landlady now."

"I had, yes," said Hylas.

"Well, your rent will be going up. I daresay you know you've been paying less than your lodgings are worth. And you"—she turned on Zo—"are going to begin pulling your weight around here, or you'll have to leave. Straton wanted me to get rid of you, you know, but I argued with him. 'He's sick,' I said—as if I ever believed that. But you need to make up your mind—either you're an invalid or you're not, you can't be fine one day and then too ill to get up the next, people will notice and think we're *all* a bunch of frauds."

"I barely leave my room as it is!" Zo snapped back at her. "I let Ahmos carry me everywhere. What else do you want me to do?"

She drew a breath and then closed her mouth as if realizing whatever she'd been about to say wouldn't answer him properly. Maybe she'd been expecting him to protest—again

73

—that he wasn't *pretending* to be ill, but he'd given up on that.

"I want you to start entertaining in your room," she said. "Make the place respectable so you can have guests in there —and out here, too. It's absurd that the two of you have this courtyard all to yourselves. Get a garland from a respectable patron. Talk to Chrestos if you need instructions. Some men may think you're prettier than he is, but I don't see it myself."

She cast one more unfriendly look on Hylas, then swept out of the garden, back through Zo's room, and he could hear his door slamming behind her. He stood rooted, feeling tears gathering shamefully in his eyes and not daring to look at Hylas. Why had Hylas had to witness that scene? Couldn't Zo have been spared that?

He heard the rustling of leaves as Hylas came down from the slope where he had been digging. Maybe he would go in, discreetly leaving Zo alone. Zo couldn't tell whether he wanted that or not.

"Is there anything I can do to help?" Hylas asked. He wasn't leaving.

"What could you do?" The words came out snappishly, to Zo's shame.

"I don't know," said Hylas. "That's why I asked. I—I don't know whether I should pretend not to have heard what she said to you, but I don't think you're malingering the way she suggested."

"No?"

"I don't know what's hard to understand about it. Some days you're steady on your feet and some days you're not. Illnesses can be like that."

Zo drew a long breath and let it out. It was so simple, but it helped more than he could have imagined to hear Hylas say this.

"I'm sure she'd have no trouble understanding if she

didn't dislike me to begin with." He ran a hand over his eyes, which had remained dry, and turned to smile at Hylas.

"I—I would help, if there was anything … "

Zo laughed wryly. "Go looking through town for men who might like me and bring them to the house, I suppose. After checking to see whether they're rich, of course."

"Of course. Did she, er, say something about tidying your room? Perhaps I could help with that."

"What? No, it's not tidying it needs, it's … I don't know, redecorating? I'll show you."

Hylas followed him inside and stood looking around the room.

"This is clever, what you've done here," he said, pointing at the hooks along the wall. He walked up and inspected one. "How did you anchor them in the wall? I see, that looks solid. Nice work."

"Thanks."

"Something else you might think of doing—I did something similar for my mother, when she had arthritis in her knees. If you can raise the bed up a little, it makes it easier to get in and out. I don't know if it's your knees that give you trouble, or … And you can put a rail on the wall, to hold onto. Well, you have that chair there. Smart." He frowned, looking around again. "So what's the problem?"

"I think all the things you've just pointed out are the problem. It looks too much like an invalid's room and not enough like a companion's."

Hylas rolled his eyes. "I'll add that to my list of things I'm looking for in a patron for you. I'll find you somebody who won't care."

CHAPTER 8

"Are you Loukianos's new man, then?"

"I ... I beg your pardon?"

Hylas looked at the companion who had sat down beside him. They were at the Bower of Suos that evening, Loukianos was on the other side of the room deep in conversation with some other guests, and Hylas had been sitting by himself. The young man who had taken the cushion beside him was strikingly handsome, with bronze skin and crisply curling black hair. His expression was politely unfriendly.

"I heard the two of you went for a walk on the Eastern Beach," he said, "and a refreshing dip in the sea. He's been talking about it. I suppose, odd as it seems, you must be his new man."

It took Hylas another moment of staring stupidly to grasp what the companion meant. He thought Hylas and Loukianos were lovers.

"Did—did he say that I was?" That would be a bizarre twist.

"No, of course not. I can put two and two together."

"I—I daresay you can. But, um ... " He tried to think what Zo would say, under these circumstances. He'd had a week's worth of conversations with Zo over breakfast by this time to gather examples. "You seem to have arrived at three?" he managed.

The companion blinked at him, then gave a bright, surprised laugh. "Oh! I do beg your pardon, then. And I can't say I'm sorry to hear it," he added, becoming much more friendly. "One has always hoped to catch the governor's eye, you know. It's only natural."

Hylas guessed it would be, if you were one of only a small number of male companions in town, and knew—as apparently everyone did—that the governor liked men.

The governor liked men. Hylas hadn't realized that, but he should have. Loukianos's favourite tea house was the one that was half male companions.

"Does he … need a new man? Not that I'm, er, in the running, but … " He was thinking along different lines entirely.

The companion shrugged. "If he hasn't told you about Hippolytos, I probably shouldn't gossip, though I think it was quite common knowledge. He had a lover, there was a tragic death." He waved a hand as if talking about such things was beneath him, or maybe just didn't suit the image he cultivated as one of the Bower's companions. "But that was well over a year ago now."

Could it really be this easy? Had he already found the perfect patron for Zo? They could even talk about gardening together.

And Loukianos was a decent man. He would treat Zo well, be careful with him if they … when they …

And maybe they would be so happy together that they would both think fondly of Hylas ever afterward, as the man who brought them together. That was a kind of happiness that someone like him could be worthy of.

"What are you doing over here by yourself?"

The governor's friend Timon appeared in front of Hylas

apparently from nowhere. Hylas realized he *was* by himself, because the companion he had been talking to had melted away, as they sometimes did when you sat stupidly lost in your own thoughts for too long.

"This place is dead tonight," Timon complained. "None of the good-looking girls are even here. Where's Loukianos? We should go somewhere else."

"We could go to the Red Balconies," said Hylas eagerly.

Timon gave him a quizzical look. "Really? What's there that's worth seeing these days? I've heard it's dull. Whatsisname used to have a mistress there, but even he admitted the place had gone downhill."

"I-it's a nice place, I think. They have very good musicians, and they serve delicious food."

"Mm. They ought to be a restaurant, not a tea house."

Hylas surprised himself by laughing. "If that would stop you enjoying yourself, I suppose you'd better not go."

The look Timon was giving him became even more quizzical. But Loukianos reappeared at that point, and the conversation was mercifully dropped. The party agreed to leave for the Amber Lily, and Hylas produced a very convincing yawn and said it was time for him to head home.

On the walk, his thoughts returned to his conversation with that companion at the Bower of Suos and the possibility of Loukianos becoming Zo's patron. It shouldn't be too hard to get the governor himself to go to the Red Balconies. His friends might turn up their noses, but Loukianos had promised to show Hylas around all the tea houses, and so long as Hylas didn't let on that he was actually living at the House of the Red Balconies, they should be able to get there eventually.

But something else occurred to Hylas. That companion had thought *he* was Loukianos's lover. Did that mean that the last man Loukianos had been with had been someone like him—older than Zo, closer to Loukianos's own age?

Would he even be drawn to Zo? Just because he liked men
…

But that was absurd. No one who liked men could fail to be drawn to Zo. He was young, but he was not a boy; he was erudite and eloquent, like all the companions. And even before you got to know him, you couldn't fail to be captivated. He was so lovely: all that tumbled dark hair, the quick grace of his hands, that deep, dark voice, like water running underground.

Even if you weren't drawn to men, as Hylas wasn't …

He stopped dead in the moonlit street with the force of the realization. He had been telling himself that lie for so long that it had become part of him, and he'd forgotten it *was* a lie. But he wasn't in Ariata now. He was on Tykanos, where even the governor could have a male lover and no one seemed to bat an eyelash.

Of course he liked men. He always had. It had been part of the shame that had poisoned his life in Ariata, where you were allowed to have sex with men but not to admit that you liked it, or something—he'd never understood it, though it had seemed so obvious to everyone else. He'd just buried that part of himself, so far down that he had forgotten it was there.

He walked the rest of the way home in a daze, forgetting to return to the question of whether Loukianos would like Zo or not.

The mood at the Red Balconies that night was very bleak. "Dire" was how Chrestos described it in an aside to Pani and Zo. Captain Themistokles was away at sea, so he was thrown upon the mercy of the regular guests like the rest of them. No one felt much sympathy for him.

It was almost too cold to be still entertaining in the

courtyard, but the sitting rooms were not yet ready for guests. Everyone put on warm clothes and hoped for the best.

Mistress Aula had been threatening everyone all week. Pani and Menthe were the worst off; Mistress had inherited their contracts with the house, and as good as owned them now. She had told both of them flatly that if they didn't find patrons before Turning Month, she would sell them to a Gylphian brothel. Theano had tried to tell them that she wouldn't really do it, as she would lose money, but that wasn't much comfort. Pani reported having heard Mistress making some threat to Theano herself, or at least talking to her in what Pani interpreted as a threatening tone. There had been a shouting match between Mistress and Taris over Taris's head-scarves, which Mistress had long disliked almost as much as Zo's crutch—Taris had beautifully thick, creamy-blonde hair which Mistress felt the guests had "a right" to see. For now, the headscarf was still in place, but Taris—normally Mistress's loyalest supporter—had a hard look in her eyes that showed the argument had taken its toll.

Some of Zo's regular guests, a group of marines, were there that evening, and they were in poor spirits themselves. He got them talking, in the ways that he knew how, and learned that they were worried about a possible action on the Deshan Coast. He listened and asked sympathetic questions as if he knew of the places and powers they named only by rumour; this allowed them to show off their knowledge, distracting them from their worry. In fact, though he'd never been to the Deshan Coast himself, always confined further inland, he knew all about the situation there. Or what it had been five years ago, though it didn't sound as though it had changed much.

"You always know how to lift our spirits, Zo," said one of the marines after they had persuaded him to sing for them.

"It's an honour," Zo replied, but he felt a wave of sadness. He wished he had someone to lift *his* spirits just then.

Hylas came in, having obviously left another tea house early, his usual habit. He looked lost in thought. Chrestos bounced over to talk to him, foolishly, and Zo saw Mistress Aula notice and approach, frowning. He winced, wishing that he could catch Hylas's eye and warn him.

"You have to pay like everyone else! Don't think you're special!" Her voice could be heard all over the courtyard. An embarrassed hush fell.

Hylas made some flustered reply, Chrestos tried to intervene and clearly only made matters worse, and it ended with Hylas hastening over to the incense burner.

"What did he do to warrant that?" one of Zo's guests wondered aloud.

"He looks harmless," another one agreed with a laugh.

"Bit of a dragon, your mistress, isn't she?"

Gossiping about Mistress was a sure path to more trouble, so Zo did his best to pretend he hadn't heard, offering his guests more wine and producing the first innocuous topic of conversation that came to mind. Hylas, he saw out of the corner of his eye, had lit a stick of incense and gone straight out of the courtyard to his room.

"And she thinks *we're* the problem. We're not the problem—she is. Do you know why the sitting rooms aren't ready and everyone had to freeze in the courtyard last night? It's because she decided to start redecorating, yesterday. Everything's torn up. And we can't afford that. It's true the rooms were looking shabby, but I don't know where that money's going to come from. And then she goes off at the aqueduct man like that—tch. I don't know what's going to become of us."

Hylas stood paralyzed in the kitchen door, waiting for the cook, who had seen him, to point out to Theano that he was there. She did so finally, with a wry smile, when Theano stopped for breath.

"Immortal gods, Elpis, you shouldn't have let me go on like that. Hello, Hylas."

Theano was sitting on a stool at the table where Elpis was kneading dough. Her baby—Hylas hadn't yet learned its name—was in her lap, playing with a wooden spoon.

"Good morning," said Hylas. He should probably ignore everything he had overheard; that would be the polite thing. "I don't usually see you up so early."

"Leta is getting a tooth and not sleeping well. I'll go back to bed when she lets me."

"Do you like babies?" Elpis asked Hylas. "Tuma, start getting the aqueduct man's tea ready, will you?"

"Oh yes. I have a niece and nephew back ... um, where I'm from. I used to like visiting them."

"Don't get home much?" Theano said.

"Give him the baby," Elpis suggested. "Sit and have a cuddle," she advised Hylas, gesturing with a floury hand at another stool. "Cheers everyone up."

"I'm not in nearly as much need of cheering up as the rest of you," said Hylas, then thought that had effectively broken his resolve of not mentioning what he had overheard. "Er, I mean ... "

"We know what you mean," said Elpis.

Hylas took a seat at the end of the worktable, and Theano passed him the baby. She was so small and soft, looking up bright-eyed at Hylas, her little mouth open, still clutching her wooden spoon in one tiny hand. Hylas nestled her in the crook of his arm, remembering what it had been like to hold his sister Maia's children at this age.

"I haven't been back to where I'm from in five years. I should go, someday soon, but my sister and her kids are the only things I miss."

"So Mistress Aula hasn't threatened you with eviction?" said Theano after a moment.

"Er, no. She has said that she'll raise my rent, but to be honest, that's fair. I'd been thinking myself the rooms are worth more than I pay for them."

Theano sighed. "I know. The house hasn't been … " She hesitated. "Oh, what does it matter. You've already heard me speaking frankly. The house hasn't been run properly in years. She just doesn't care enough. We'd had misfortunes when the late landlord bought this place, but we could have recovered if he and Aula had worked together sensibly."

"He should have put Theano in charge," said Elpis, nodding decisively.

"I was much too young at the time. And not foolish enough to start a rivalry with the landlord's woman." She sighed. "I don't know that it's made any difference."

"She knows you'd have been a better mistress," Elpis said, "and she hates you for it." She gave her dough a final punch. "Ah well. At least she's not evicting the aqueduct man. That's good to hear."

"Zo must be glad," said Theano.

"A-ah? Yes?"

"He says you're a good neighbour."

"Right. Yes. Well, I try to be."

He might not have a better chance than this to ask a question that had been nagging at him for some time now.

"Is Zo … free?"

Theano showed no sign of thinking it an odd question; but then, she was a companion.

"Oh, absolutely. He's not indentured to the house, or anybody's slave. As far as I know he never has been."

"I see!" Hylas couldn't hide that he was glad to hear it.

"But," Theano went on, "he has nowhere else to go, no family on the island or any other way to support himself. He could go to another tea house, but with his health the way it is, I don't know if many of them would take him."

"Oh," said Hylas. "I … I see."

"So when Mistress Aula, for instance, tells him that he's got to find a man to give him a garland—as she's been telling all of us—no, she can't compel him, she doesn't own him. But she could turn him out of the house, and it would be bad for him. That's what you were wondering, I guess?"

"Yes, I—yes, I suppose so."

His tea was ready, and he returned the baby to her mother and carried the tray back to his room as usual. And yet everything felt different that morning. What he had realized last night had changed the very quality of the air and the light. He felt more alive, somehow.

And he was also slightly nervous about being near Zo again, knowing what he now knew about himself. Would he see Zo differently? Would it be easier or harder to look at him?

He got back to his room, took the tray out into the garden, as usual, and found that Zo was not yet up. This was the first time, since they started breakfasting together in the garden, that this had happened, and Hylas stood with the tray in his hands for a few moments, unsure what to do about it.

Finally he put the tray down, went to the screen over Zo's doorway, and knocked softly.

"Hylas?" came Zo's sleepy voice from inside.

"Are you up?"

"Yeah … no. Come in, though."

Hylas slid the screen half-open and looked around it. Zo was sitting up in bed, hair tousled, eyes closed to slits against the light. His robe was open down the front, and Hylas could see a slice of smooth, bare chest.

"I'll bring your breakfast in," Hylas suggested, "and you eat when you feel like it."

"Oh." Zo smiled sleepily. "That's nice of you, Hylas."

Hylas filled one of the bowls with tea, put the buns for his own breakfast on the tray, and brought the bowl and the basket of buns in to set on the chair beside Zo's bed. Zo was lying down again. There were dark smudges under his eyes that were not from his makeup.

"Don't let the tea get cold," Hylas advised, and went back out, sliding the screen shut behind him.

It felt the same, after all. Nothing had changed; he had just awoken to how things really were. Hylas smiled to himself as he sat in the sun outside Zo's door and drank his own tea.

CHAPTER 9

"I'm sorry," Mutari said as she showed Hylas into one of the small, glittering, daytime sitting rooms at the House of the Peacock. "I wish I had good news for you. But it's become complicated, I'm afraid."

"I appreciate your help," said Hylas quickly. "I hope this isn't—hasn't been—too much trouble for you."

"Not at all." She seated herself, arranging the folds of her dress. He took the couch opposite her. The table between them was covered in a clutter of papers and scrolls rather than dishes of food. "I'm as eager as everyone else for that aqueduct to be built. Especially now that more visitors are coming to the island. But the difficulty is that the Glifian envoy has just been recalled."

"Oh. That … sounds bad."

"Yes, it's terrible timing for us, although it was only to be expected, since the change of regime in Tetum. If only I'd come back from my trip a few days sooner, I might have been able to do something about this before he received the letter —we could have sneaked it in." She shook her head regretfully. "I'm truly sorry."

"What? But, immortal gods, it's not your fault. If this

were—I mean, in most places, surely, I'd have been able to go to see the Gylphian envoy myself and put the case before him, instead of the—the roundabout way that … "

He trailed off, afraid of being rude. It wasn't that he thought she *shouldn't* be an integral part of getting engineering projects approved on the island, just because she was a woman, or a companion. Or, well, maybe on some level he did think that, and he realized he didn't want to.

"It isn't exactly direct," she agreed, smoothing her skirt with her lacquered fingernails. "And it can be inefficient. But it is how the women who populate the houses which bring most of the wealth to this island can have a say in the island's fate. It isn't as if we can vote in any assembly." She laughed gently. "Even the men of Tykanos can barely do that. Our governor is appointed by Pheme, and the army and navy control everything else. The only things decided by the local assembly are where to dump the rubbish and who is in charge of cleaning the streets."

"I understand," said Hylas, and he hoped she could see he was trying. "I—I just want you to have your aqueduct."

"I'll tell you what. I will write to some people I know in Tetum who are close to the court. They'll be able to tell me if a new envoy has been appointed yet and what is known of him—that way I will be able to begin planning in advance how to approach him." She looked at him from under her lashes. "You know. Who might catch his eye, and so on."

If she was trying to make him blush—and he thought she probably was—she succeeded. "I hope—that is, I hate to think of any woman having to s-sacrifice herself in any way to—to—that is, if there's anything I can do … "

She shrugged elegantly. "If he likes older redheads, I will certainly let you know."

Hylas must have been beet-red by this time, to judge by the heat of his face, but to his surprise he could also laugh.

87

"Let us hope you don't have to, er, to rely on me in th-that way," he managed.

"I have been inhospitable this morning," she said, sitting up straight on her couch. "Forgive me. I have not offered you tea." She reached for the clutter on the table and began gathering things up.

"Oh, that's all right. I had tea at home before I left. I—I lodge at the Red Balconies."

"*Do* you? Is Theano still there? I haven't seen her in so long. But perhaps you don't talk to the girls."

"No, I—I do know all the companions there a little. Theano is there. She ... she has a child. Leta. She is ... " He didn't know the baby's age, so he held his hands apart an appropriate amount. "About this big."

"Truly! I didn't know."

"Perhaps I shouldn't have told you."

"No, no. Theano and I were good friends, before Aula took over the Red Balconies and forbade any of their girls from coming here. We used to visit each other and even host together, you know. But that's very different now—not entirely because of Aula, customs have just changed, but it's certainly true that she bears everyone at the Peacock a grudge because she felt she never got her due here." Mutari rolled her eyes. "So Theano has a little girl. How I would like to see her!"

Hylas's mind was filled with schemes for how they might arrange a meeting. He could find out when Theano was going to the market, for instance—surely she must sometimes go out to the market—and bring a message to Mutari. Then his gaze fell on one of the scrolls on her table, and he read the tag on it.

"Is that a copy of *The Bronze Dolphin*?"

"Oh, yes. It's so good. Have you read it?"

"No, but I've heard of it."

"This one's mine. Would you like to borrow it?"

He hesitated, remembering what Zo had said about the tea houses not lending each other books. If she knew that he was taking it to share with other companions—well, specifically with Zo—but she already knew he lived at the Red Balconies, and she was friends with Theano.

"I think you'll like it," she said, misinterpreting his silence. "There's a couple in it, Tyreus and Nikostratos—their love story is beautifully told."

Surely those were two men's names? Hylas eyed the scroll with renewed interest. He had thought he wanted to borrow it just for Zo, but perhaps he would read it himself.

Mutari was smiling at him. "I thought you might like that," she said, pulling the scroll out of the pile and offering it to him.

"I—I—why?" he stalled. "Why did you think I would like … that?"

She reached across the table and tossed the scroll so that it landed in his lap. "Sometimes I can just tell. Men like you and Loukianos are a great boon to women like me, you know."

"W-we are?" He'd have thought it was the opposite.

"Oh, yes. One can't do all one's politicking in bed. It's handy to have men to deal with who don't expect it."

After that, Hylas would have liked to rush home with the book to show Zo, but as it happened he had work to do at the government office and was occupied there the rest of the day. It was late afternoon by the time he was ready to leave, but it was with the satisfaction, rare these days, of having actually been able to do a good day's work. He had hoped that Loukianos would come in so that he could ask about his salary, which, with the new rent he was going to have to pay, was becoming more urgent, but you couldn't have everything.

On the walk home, he imagined offering the scroll of *The Bronze Dolphin* to Zo, telling him the story of how he'd come to borrow it, maybe hinting at the reason Mutari had suggested he would like it. At that, he laughed aloud in the street, thinking of the shade of red he would turn if he tried any such thing. It didn't matter. Zo would like that aspect of the story himself, and it would be a pleasure just to watch him read.

Of course he would have to wait until the following morning, because Zo would be at work now. Today Hylas would go sit with him; he could afford one more stick of incense, and he wouldn't stupidly leave as he had last week.

Later, he would talk to Zo about inviting the governor. He wouldn't say that he was hoping Loukianos would fall for Zo, because he wanted that to be a surprise. But he also wanted Zo to know, when it happened, that it had been he, Hylas, who had planned it.

Everyone was still in the courtyard when Hylas arrived. It really was too cold for this now, and there were only a few guests. They had lit a brazier and were huddled around it, listening to Pani play her harp. Hylas hid *The Bronze Dolphin* under his cloak and was about to head for the incense burner when he saw one of the guests wave in his direction, looked, and registered who it was.

Timon, the armourer. He was sitting next to Zo, and when he lowered the hand he'd used to wave at Hylas, it came to rest on Zo's thigh. Hylas saw Timon look down, as if he'd done that by accident, then up into Zo's face, not moving his hand. Zo slid his fingers under Timon's palm and flicked his hand away, as delicately as he might have done a fallen leaf, smiling into Timon's eyes as he did. It was such a lovely thing, Hylas wanted to see it again. What was the word for that?

Flirtatious. He'd never seen Zo so openly flirtatious before.

Well. Timon was a good choice for a patron, certainly. He was very rich, influential, and established on the island. Hylas didn't like him, but that didn't matter. Maybe Zo would like him. Maybe that didn't matter either.

It would be a shame, though, because Hylas was pretty sure Zo *would* have liked Governor Loukianos.

Zo could see Mistress Aula radiating approval from across the cold courtyard, and he knew that someone must have told her who the man sitting next to him was. Or perhaps she'd just known him by sight; she went into town, after all.

Zo had vaguely heard of him, but had pretended he hadn't when the man sat down beside him and introduced himself. Timon of Kos, the armourer: the soldiers mentioned him occasionally, not to say anything in particular about the man, just that they'd bought such-and-such blade at Timon's shop, or were saving up for such-and-such spear or helmet or piece of equipment that Zo had never heard of, and Timon of Kos was holding it for them.

Obviously he did well for himself. He wore a big gold ring with a lapis lazuli seal—Zo *did* know about that sort of thing—and his tunic and mantle were the kind of flawless, almost glowing white that meant they were either brand new or had been expensively cleaned in the very recent past. He was balding, so he'd had his head completely shaved—fault-lessly, his barber must have been expensive too—and wore a full, carefully groomed dark beard.

Zo let him talk about himself and his business, showing only a polite interest, which was what he calculated would work better with a man like this than fawning awe. It was a gamble, because the man gave little of his personality away at a first meeting, and most of what he had told Zo so far was as factual as what Zo had already learned from the soldiers. But the gambit seemed to be working. Timon did not budge from Zo's side, barely stopped looking at him, and eventually Zo began to detect a subtle hunger in his gaze.

That wasn't necessarily good. Sex was not what Zo sold, and though there had been times when it had suited his purposes to get a man into bed quickly, this wasn't one of them. He needed Timon of Kos to stay hungry, and Timon seemed like he was probably the kind of man who wasn't accustomed to doing that.

He wore a heavy scent—frankincense and cinnamon, if Zo was any judge, which he was—probably to cover the unpleasant smell of all the freshly laundered wool he had on. He was leaning in close to Zo now, and waved at someone. Zo followed the direction of the wave and saw to his astonishment that the person Timon was greeting was Hylas.

Why was he surprised? Hylas went out in the town, visited the other tea houses, must have known all sorts of people. He had been personally hired by the governor. He was the Aqueduct Man, the hero of Koilas. Of course someone like Timon of Kos might know him.

Just because Zo only ever saw him in the seclusion of their shared garden or the courtyard of the Red Balconies didn't mean that was Hylas's whole world, the way it was Zo's.

He was so distracted by these thoughts that he almost didn't notice Timon's hand landing on his leg. He flicked it off instinctively while tossing Timon an encouraging smile.

Hylas lit his incense and returned, looking tentative, to take a seat at the brazier across from Zo and Timon.

"I might have known I would see you here, Hylas," Timon said lazily. To Zo he added, "Hylas was the one who convinced me to come to the Red Balconies. Though he did not mention that this old ruin of a house was concealing a treasure such as yourself. But he may not have an eye for the finer things, as I do. Eh, Hylas?"

"Hm?" said Hylas, which was so exactly what Zo would have said if he'd wanted to avoid either agreeing or disagreeing with a guest that he wanted to laugh.

Or maybe to cry, because this man clearly wasn't Hylas's friend; he was a condescending acquaintance whom Hylas had taken pains to send Zo's way, just as he had said he would. Zo had been joking when he'd asked Hylas to do it, and he'd thought Hylas had been joking when he said he would. But he'd really done it. Zo owed it to him to make the most of the opportunity.

So they sat around the brazier in the chilly courtyard, and Zo flirted carefully with Timon, watching the hunger in the armourer's eyes building. He played Timon off against Hylas, daringly, by paying more attention to the aqueduct man for a bit, to see if that would engender a spark of jealousy in Timon—it did—and all the while Hylas watched Zo with naked admiration. As if he was simply enjoying Zo's technique. It lifted Zo's spirits in a way nothing else could have done, made him feel he could have gone on talking and pouring wine and laughing elegantly at Timon's barely-passable witticisms all night without getting tired, provided Hylas was there to appreciate it. This man who knew how to build bridges and aqueducts and save towns from flooding—really useful things—somehow was impressed with the useless fluff that was Zo's whole stock in trade, and it was the best feeling in the world.

Timon left in the early hours of the morning, after having several times, at intervals, remarked that he had an important meeting the next day and needed his sleep. He looked deeply unsatisfied, when he left, in the best possible way.

Hylas had put the crowning glory on Zo's achievement by falling asleep, leaning against a pillar and wrapped in his cloak like a soldier on a night watch. Zo reached over and shook him gently by the shoulder after Timon was gone.

"Hm?" Hylas's eyes popped open, unfocussed. "Oh dear, I really fell asleep, didn't I?"

"You certainly did." Zo gave him an arch look which seemed to roll right off him.

"I was, well, pretending at first. I thought you might want an opportunity to say something about how late it was, and oh look, poor Hylas has gone to sleep, how I envy him." He grimaced. "Gods, I shouldn't try to help you like this, should I? I've no idea what I'm doing, and you're an expert."

He'd had, if Zo was any judge—and he was—too much wine to be called quite sober. But it looked good on him. He seemed relaxed and happy.

"It was perfect," Zo said. "Timon hated to be the first to leave, but I hinted I thought you were drunk, and that made him feel good about himself because he wasn't, and he didn't want to have to offer to see you home if you woke up, so he left, feeling jealous that you got to stay."

"Goodness. So I did well?"

"You can help me any time. Speaking of which, how about helping me up right now?"

Hylas obediently scrambled to his feet. As he did, something tumbled out of his lap and rolled into the torchlight. It was a scroll, and the writing on the label caught Zo's eye.

"*The Bronze Dolphin*! Where did you get that?"

"Oh, I'd forgotten it altogether." Hylas stooped to pick it up and presented it to Zo, smiling. "I borrowed it for you. I can't tell you where, and I want to read it too, but I'll let you have it first."

"You beautiful man," said Zo.

Hylas laughed aloud as he grasped Zo's forearms and hauled him carefully to his feet.

CHAPTER 10

THE NEXT MORNING was too cold for sitting in the garden. Zo woke late with a headache and a vague memory of Hylas visiting on his way out and leaving tea. It was lukewarm now, but the buns were still good. He ate them sitting in bed and brushed the crumbs off the blanket.

It had been a while since he'd had a truly late night; evenings had been ending early at the Red Balconies, a symptom of the lack of guests. He hadn't realized how much he'd begun to count on the extra sleep.

Mistress Aula was still pleased with him. She told everyone so that morning, breezing into the companions' sitting room to announce that they should all follow Zo's example.

"Mistress," Menthe ventured meekly, "where are we going to entertain tonight? It's too cold for the courtyard ... "

"In your rooms, of course. You should be spending more time with the guests in your rooms anyway."

"Surely we can get the good winter sitting room ready for tonight," said Theano, "if we work together."

"What? Don't be impertinent! None of the furnishings

I've ordered are ready. You'll meet your guests in the court-yard and bring them back to your rooms."

"That hasn't been the custom of the house," said Theano.

"I don't care! It is now! And you'll all get yourselves garlands from rich patrons. If Zo and Chrestos can do it, the rest of you can, too. I'm not having my house thought of as a place where you come to court boys—not when I have perfectly good girls on offer."

"I like how she managed to make that sound like an insult to you too, somehow," Menthe remarked to Zo after Mistress had gone.

He winced. "Did you notice that? I noticed that."

"There's no winning with her," said Pani grimly. "Do you know she tried to pull Taris's headscarf off last night? She only stopped because one of the guests saw her."

"And she yelled at the aqueduct man last week in front of guests," Menthe added.

Theano sighed. "I'll try to reason with her again, though I'm afraid she won't listen to me. If I can at least get her to compromise on some of the redecorating, we can have a usable sitting room, and that will be something."

"Won't we risk losing guests if we try to take them all back to our rooms?" said Zo. "They don't all come here to see just one of us."

"Exactly." Theano rubbed her forehead. "We'll just have to do our best. Let's get on with our chores, everyone."

Hylas came into the government office to find it was payday. A pair of soldiers from the fort were there, accompanying a man from the purser's office who was handing out money and ticking off names in a ledger. Most of the staff of the office had already received their pay, but there was still a queue of others waiting their turn.

"Should I line up?" Hylas asked, uncertain because this was not the way it had worked before.

"Oh," said Dorios, one of the clerks. "I don't know. Are you on the naval payroll? I wouldn't have thought you were."

"I've never dealt with anyone from the fort before," Hylas agreed. Indeed, he'd been happy to have it that way. "But … "

"But you haven't been paid in a while?" Dorios winced. "I wondered about that, actually. We got one payment for you directly from the governor, shortly after you arrived, but we haven't had anything else. You're not in the budget."

"Oh," said Hylas. "What does that mean?"

"Probably that the governor is paying you out of his own purse. That first amount he gave you didn't go through our ledgers either. The rest of us get paid by the navy, but I think you're just working directly for Governor Loukianos."

Something about the way he said this, with a slightly apologetic tone, made Hylas uneasy.

"You'll have to go talk to him about it, I'm afraid," Dorios said. "He's probably just forgotten to pay you."

This was just what Hylas had been hoping he could avoid. He didn't want to demand pay for work that he hadn't been doing—through no fault of his own, but still. He needed to pay rent, though.

Loukianos didn't seem to be coming into the office that day, so Hylas made his way up the mountain to the governor's mansion. He found Loukianos in his garden, and that provided an excuse to talk about something other than his nonexistent salary.

"Of course I'd be happy to show you my autumn routine, but … " Loukianos's smile was puzzled. "Why?"

"Oh, I've been doing some work in the garden of—the garden at my lodgings. My neighbour planted it, but he's not always well enough to tend it, so I've been helping him."

"Ah! Good man. And so you want some pointers?"

"Yes, I just thought I might be more use to him if I knew what I was doing. And, er, if I were able to make some suggestions for improvement ... " He shrugged, embarrassed.

Loukianos's eyebrows rose. "Say no more. This neighbour is someone you want to impress, clearly. Is there a beautiful daughter, or ... please say it's not a neglected wife."

"What? Oh! No no no—nothing of the sort, no, please don't worry. I—I want to be a good friend, that's all."

That was true, but it also felt inadequate. The truth was, he felt a desire to repay Zo for something. What, exactly? Perhaps just for the beauty that Zo had brought into his life. Perhaps there was no better way of putting it.

He couldn't help thinking again, as he followed Loukianos through the governor's garden, listening to his description of all the work that needed to be done to prepare for winter, that it was a shame he couldn't introduce Zo and Loukianos.

In the end, Hylas never did ask about his salary, but it was Loukianos who brought up the subject. In a way.

"I've been meaning to ask," he said, "do you need any cash?"

"Er, well, I ... "

"My dear fellow, you've only to say! I'll arrange some-thing, not to worry. Any time you need a sum, just let me know. Better yet, you know you may always charge things to my account, anywhere on the island."

"Thank you, sir. That is very generous of you."

It was generous. It was also not at all the way Hylas wanted to proceed. He realized now, as he should have seen a long time ago, that the reason no salary had been mentioned when he first took this job was because Loukianos didn't think in those terms. Maybe he thought Hylas was a man of independent means. Or maybe his idea was that Hylas would be his dependent, living off his bounty while the aqueduct project was in progress. He probably didn't think in terms of paying rent, either, and if Hylas mentioned that his rent had recently increased, he'd find himself invited to move into the governor's mansion. Hylas didn't want that at all.

They went to the Amber Lily again that night, and Hylas tried to be pleased when the companion who had gossiped about the governor's lover before attached himself to Loukianos and engaged him in conversation most of the evening. Perhaps they would both be happier for it; perhaps this young man would, after all, suit Loukianos better than Zo. Hylas noticed that Timon wasn't there.

He'd had a chance to think about it more, and he'd decided that Loukianos's failure to pay him a salary was likely deliberate. The governor wanted the aqueduct to be seen as his gift to the island; he couldn't make that point so effectively by simply putting an engineer on the navy's payroll. He needed Hylas to be his man, his crony, in some kind of patronage relationship with him. He probably wouldn't have minded if he'd known that he and Hylas were rumoured to be a couple.

The courtyard of the Red Balconies was empty when he arrived home, the first time that had happened. It was bitterly cold.

"They're all entertaining in their rooms," Ahmos told him as Hylas stood looking around in surprise.

"Oh. How's that going?"

The bouncer shrugged. "It's a shitshow. Guests have been leaving without waiting for an explanation, people think we're closed or got plague in the house or something. We're short-staffed in the kitchen, and the girls have had to run back and forth for food all evening. Nah, it's a disaster."

"Gods. I'm sorry. At least the winter doesn't last long."

"Yeah, we might pull through."

The walls of the house were thick, and Hylas couldn't hear much from Zo's room, just the occasional extra-loud burst of laughter. He couldn't guess how many guests Zo might be entertaining, and he tried not to spend too much time thinking about it. He had known this was an aspect of Zo taking a patron that might cause disruption to his routine, but he had no right at all to complain about it.

He tapped very tentatively at Zo's garden door the following morning. It was cold enough now that the screens were supplemented by solid sliding shutters. He could hear sounds from inside, so he knew Zo was up, but had no idea whether he was alone or not.

"Come in," said Zo's voice, with an unhappy edge to it.

Hylas slid open the shutter and then the lattice inside it. Zo was standing on a chair, half-dressed, at the wall where he hung his clothes and jewellery. Everything was piled on the floor, and he was tugging at one of the hooks in the wall. He stopped and looked down at Hylas.

"What are you doing?" Hylas asked, trying not to sound alarmed. He set down his tray on the end of Zo's unmade bed.

"I have to change the room," said Zo, gesturing expansively and wobbling on the chair. "I have to take these down. Timon said it looked like a storeroom and I 'deserve better.'"

"You brought him to your room." Hylas hoped he didn't sound like a disapproving parent. He took a step closer to the chair, ready to catch Zo if he fell.

"I had to— Mistress told us we had to entertain in our rooms, because the sitting rooms aren't ready and the courtyard is too cold. I had a half dozen guests last night, and I had to bring them all back here. It was awful. There was nowhere sensible for them to sit, and they went on about what a bad room it is and how hard-done-by I am. Timon said, 'This is where they keep you? They don't value you highly enough.' I'm afraid he'll say something to Mistress about it, and she'll move me to a different room. I'd lose my garden."

"Stop," said Hylas firmly. "You won't lose your garden.

As long as I'm in my rooms, you can get to it any time you want. But let's make sure it doesn't come to that. Don't take those out of the wall, though. You won't be able to get them back in—you're making the hole bigger—and it's going to look messy. We'll put up curtains and cover all this."

"That's ... a good idea." Zo frowned, as if he had expected to be able to find fault with Hylas's suggestion but couldn't.

He climbed down from the chair and sat on it. He was wearing the trousers that he wore to work in the garden, and a short jacket open at the front with no tunic or shirt under it. Hylas tried not to look at his bare chest.

Hylas went on: "I'll take down the curtains in my room and bring them over. I may need to run out and buy some hooks to hang them, but I should be able to have them up for you by this evening."

"Hylas! You can't just give me your curtains."

He started, ready to be mortified. Surely there wasn't some taboo about curtains? "Can I not?"

Zo groaned. "I don't mean you *can't*—I mean how can I accept them? You just bought them for yourself."

It was Hylas's turn to frown. "If you would prefer to give me money to go to the market and buy curtains for you, I can tell you how much mine cost."

"I don't have money for curtains."

"I know you don't."

Hylas's own curtains had been an extravagant expense, all those yards of fabric, even though they were only dyed a modest shade of cheerful yellow. If he'd realized sooner that he wasn't getting a salary, he would not have bought them. But now he was glad he had.

"I don't want you to be turned out of your room, Zo. Please accept my curtains and let me hang them for you."

Zo nodded. "Of course. Thank you, Hylas."

"It's all right. We'll solve this together. Was there anything else wrong with the room?"

"Uh … it's dark? Which is because I broke my lamp and haven't replaced it. I don't know how much lamps cost … "

That was an odd thing not to know, but perhaps they used candles or something where Zo was from. "They're cheap. Much cheaper than curtains. I'll buy you one when I go to get the hooks."

"She wants me to entertain in here … I don't have any of the right furniture."

"Right. No, you don't. You need cushions for seating, a table, maybe a, er, screen or something in front of your bed. Is there extra furniture elsewhere in the house that you could borrow?"

Zo drew in a deep breath and got to his feet. He swayed and caught the back of the chair to stay upright.

"What is it?" Hylas strode toward him, hands going up instinctively.

"Dizzy spell. I—get them all the time. Half the reason why I use the crutch. I shouldn't—I was trying to do too much, and I didn't sleep well."

"Here." Hylas offered an arm, and Zo took it and let himself be led back to his bed.

He sat, then drew up his feet and lay down, curled up, looking miserable. Hylas moved the tray with the tea and buns to the floor. He filled a bowl and stood waiting with it until Zo opened his eyes.

"I'm making a lot of trouble for you this morning," Zo said unhappily.

"No. You're in need of help that I'm well able to provide. That … gives me great satisfaction."

Zo's smile dawned slow and exquisite. "Well, you're welcome, then."

He reached out a hand. Hylas tried to offer the bowl of tea, but Zo reached for his free hand instead, and for a moment just clasped Hylas's fingers. Zo's fingers were slim and cold. Surely it was the first time their hands had ever touched? Hylas returned the grasp for an instant, as long as he felt he deserved, then let go.

"Your hands are cold," he said. "You should drink some tea to warm yourself."

In the end, it was an oddly good day. Zo spent most of his time resting, while Hylas came and went, bringing in things from the marketplace and from elsewhere in the house, putting up curtains and arranging furniture. He detached the screen from the garden door and built a kind of stand for it so that it could be positioned to divide the room into a sitting area and a sleeping nook. He enlisted Theano's help, and they found cushions and a small table—it wobbled, but Hylas made it level with a wedge of folded paper, meticulously testing it until it didn't move even a little.

At lunchtime he got Zo up, and they ate with the rest of the companions. Everyone made a fuss about having the aqueduct man join them for a meal at last, and Zo felt rather smug when he thought of all the breakfasts he and Hylas had shared.

In the afternoon, as Hylas finished working on the room, Zo read aloud from *The Bronze Dolphin*. When the room had been fully transformed, curtains covering the storage on the wall, screen dividing the space, a cozy seating area created, Hylas came and sat beside Zo on his bed and took over reading. He had a flat, undramatic delivery, and for some reason, when he was reading, his Ariatan accent became stronger. Zo didn't mind. He lay back against his pillows, fantasizing about draping his legs over Hylas's lap, which was bittersweet because he knew he'd never actually do it.

CHAPTER 11

HYLAS DREW up a strict budget for himself. He allowed himself two sticks of incense at the Red Balconies each week, provided he had no other extraordinary expenses. Over the weeks that followed he began taking all his meals at home, when he wasn't dining out with the governor, to avoid expenditure on food. In this way he should be able to pay his rent for two more months with the money he had on hand, before having to beg more from Loukianos.

With Tenth Month came Dendreia, which Tykanos celebrated in the Phemian style, with gift-giving and feasts, not with the austere sacrifices and ritual combat that Hylas remembered from home. Loukianos felt the need to apologize for the small scale of the island's festivities.

"There's a very token procession, I'm afraid—it's not a big town, and only about half of the residents actually observe the rites. Everyone being from somewhere else. Though if your feast is good enough, they'll all come out to that, no matter what they observe. I've given some decent feasts in my time, but this year ... well, 'economy' is my new watchword, you know."

This was another worrying development; it was the

second or third time Loukianos had said something like this. Hylas didn't know what the problem was, and didn't want to ask, but it had confirmed the necessity for him to husband his own cash. He hadn't been fanciful in imagining that Loukianos would invite him to live at the palace to save on rent; the governor had made some passing remark to that effect already.

For Hylas, as long as he'd been able to choose for himself, Dendreia had been a time for staying at home. Attendance at the arena in Ariata was mandatory, but there was no fine; the only thing you risked was having the mark of impiety chalked on your door if the ritual patrol noticed. Usually they didn't, and if they did, he'd try to wash it off before his mother saw. There was supposed to have been a fine for doing *that*, but in the neighbourhood where they lived, no one had cared.

Walking through the town on the Market Day before the beginning of Dendreia, he stopped to look at the array of gifts for sale in the special festival stalls: small statuettes of gods and animals, decorated lamps, candles, pieces of inexpensive jewellery and poems written on little scrolls. They were items specially made for the festival, and each had some symbolic resonance; someone in Pheme had explained it to him once, and he remembered the details vaguely.

He would buy a gift for Zo, he decided. He'd never bought a Dendreia gift for anyone—it hadn't been a custom in Ariata, and in Pheme he hadn't known anyone to give a gift to—so the thought was exciting. He pored over the gifts symbolic of Orante, goddess of beauty and patron of companions. He had it narrowed down to a choice between a painted pottery bird and a bronze bell meant to be hung as a wind chime, when it finally dawned on him that Zo was one of the people Loukianos had been referring to who didn't observe the festival.

Zo was from … wherever people who looked like him

were from, or maybe somewhere else—Hylas actually had no idea because he had never asked—but he was not Pseuchaian. He never swore by any of the Pseuchaian gods. Hylas didn't know whether he even made libations at the household altar on Hesperion's Day. He would have accepted a gift graciously, Hylas was sure, but it wouldn't have been a thoughtful gesture to give him one. It wouldn't have said, "I think about you all the time," so much as "I don't pay enough attention when you talk."

So he didn't buy anything, and then, on the first morning of Dendreia, the day for gift-giving, Zo came out into the garden with a smile on his face and a parcel wrapped in a twist of paper in his hands.

"Dendreia greetings," he said, presenting it on both hands with a winsome little bow. "Oh, is something wrong?"

"I didn't get you anything."

"That's all right." He had withdrawn the parcel when Hylas hadn't taken it and stood holding it uncertainly. "Do they do this where you're from?"

"No, they don't."

"Oh. I see, I thought they did." He held up his gift with a rueful expression. "They don't do it where I'm from, either, but you may have worked that out. But I do think you'll like this. I hope you will. I had Chrestos go to the market to buy it for me."

"Thank you," said Hylas, taking the parcel. He untwisted the paper carefully.

It was a painted pottery figurine of a donkey, symbol of the smith-god Telleros, whom Phemians considered the patron of engineers. It was the kind of gift anyone could have given him; but it hadn't been given to him by anyone. It had been given by Zo. Hylas looked at it and felt an incredible happiness.

"I made Chrestos buy half a dozen of them so I could

pick the one with the best expression," Zo explained. "He took the others back."

The donkey's expression, rendered in a couple of brush-strokes, was serene and dignified. It wore a green blanket across its back, and its tail and the tips of its ears had been painted black.

"Thank you," said Hylas. "I will treasure it."

Winter came the way it often did on Tykanos, in a sudden blast of cold rain, lashing out of a grey sky that hung over the island for weeks. At the Red Balconies they lit braziers and huddled indoors. Theano succeeded in getting one of the good sitting rooms opened up, even in its half-furnished state, and she and the other women began entertaining in there. Their loyal guests made jokes about how they would endure worse for the food and entertainment on offer. Zo divided his time between the public sitting room and his own room, where Timon of Kos had become a fixture.

It was a delicate dance, keeping Timon interested enough that he might be willing to commit to offering a garland, while also making it clear to him that he wouldn't get enough of Zo to really satisfy him until he did. Taris, who was engaged in a similar dance with a First Spear of the resident marine legion, remarked one morning at chores that she sometimes felt envious of prostitutes.

"I wish I could just write him an invoice, you know?"

Once Zo would have argued with her; he'd loved the way nothing was taken for granted, nothing specifically owed in exchange for payment at the Red Balconies. It had felt like home to him, a place where he could deploy all the skills he had learned in his precarious, pampered boyhood. But that was before he'd been obliged to single-mindedly pursue a patron. Now he knew exactly what Taris meant.

None of them had secured a garland yet. Chrestos was still doing fine with Captain Themistokles, and Taris had hopes of her marine First Spear, but the other three were completely without prospects.

Most of the guests who had at first been put off by the switch to entertaining in the companions' rooms had started to come back, but the winter was always a slow time, with no ships arriving in the harbour, and it was an open secret that the house's finances were in a bad way. Hylas told Zo he'd overheard Theano arguing with Mistress Aula about buying cheaper tea and olives—insanity, Theano had said, when the quality of the food and drink were among the Red Balconies' few remaining attractions.

Now that it was too cold to sit in the garden, Zo and Hylas ate breakfast in Hylas's room. They had never talked about it; it just happened naturally on the first rainy morning. Hylas knocked on Zo's door, cloak pulled up over his head, and said, "Tea's in my room. Come over when you're ready," and Zo came. Hylas had a little table he'd built himself out of a couple of old shutters and a barrel, and he brought in Zo's chair from outside and seated himself on top of his sea chest.

"Now we're at the same height," Zo remarked, wanting—and at the same time not wanting—to ask if Hylas had built the table to chair-height instead of cushion-height for his sake.

Hylas's eyes were on the tea he was pouring. "I miss sitting at your feet," he said.

Zo laughed but did not reply, letting the statement hang in the air, as courtly a thing as any of the compliments he ever paid his guests. He felt strangely proud of Hylas when, every so often, he came up with something like that.

Hylas continued to be a hero around the Red Balconies, because while he waited for whatever machinations were necessary to get his aqueduct built, he had managed to restore water to the fountain in the courtyard. Apparently it had only been a matter of digging in the right place and repairing a broken pipe, and water was restored to the whole street. It wasn't good drinking water—they still had to go to the fountain on the corner for that—but apparently that would change when the aqueduct was built, and in the meantime it did make filling the baths easier.

They had finished reading *The Bronze Dolphin* aloud to each other by the end of Dendreia and begun to discuss what they should try to borrow next. Zo claimed he would be interested in a treatise on bridge-building if Hylas would read it to him, and although Hylas knew he was just being charming, it was still pleasant to hear. He had learned that although Zo had a grumpy side that he would never show around his guests, that didn't mean his sunny, charming manner was entirely an act. It was a real aspect of him, too.

The mood at the Red Balconies continued to be strained as winter deepened. Hylas could discern it in the way the companions spoke to him. Some of them seemed more remote, distracted; others, like Theano, had opened up to him more, accepting him as an ally. Chrestos, with all the naval officers confined to port for the winter, was taking the opportunity to sequester himself in his room with his patron as often as possible. But one morning a few days after the end of the festival, he showed up at Hylas's door.

"Come in," Hylas said, surprised. "We're eating breakfast. You can join us if you like."

"Thanks." Chrestos loosened the cloak he had been clutching around his shoulders, as Hylas had got the room to a comfortable temperature.

"Morning, Chrestos," said Zo, with his mouth full. "What's up?"

"I, uh … " Chrestos perched on the end of Hylas's sea chest. "I heard that you guys do this, and I just wanted company this morning, so I came to barge in. Nobody else is awake."

Hylas took the other end of the chest, while Zo refilled his bowl of tea and offered it to Chrestos.

"Captain Themistokles didn't stay over?" Zo asked.

"No, he's got a sore shoulder, and he's been finding my bed uncomfortable. He'll get me a new one, it's not a big problem." He cradled his bowl of tea and sipped moodily.

Hylas exchanged a glance with Zo, who returned a reassuring smile. So he too thought there was something up with Chrestos, and he would take care of trying to draw him out. That was good.

In fact, Chrestos had come prepared to talk, and didn't need any prompting.

"Can I tell you guys a secret?" he said suddenly, putting down his tea bowl.

"Of course." Hylas and Zo both said it at once.

Chrestos drew in a deep breath through his nose. "I don't really like sex. That's not the secret," he added hastily. "He already knew that." He pointed at Zo. "The secret is—and really, don't tell anybody this—neither does Captain Themistokles. We don't really … do much. It's mostly kissing and cuddling. Is that bad?"

Zo made a strangled noise. "Why—*why*—would that be bad, Chrestos? It sounds perfect."

"Really?"

"Because you've both got what you want, and that's rare. It wouldn't suit everyone."

"You?" Chrestos's eyebrows went up.

"No. Not … no. We're not talking about me."

"But don't you think … don't you need sex in order to, like, hold onto someone?"

"Um … no? People stay together even when they stop being able to have sex, and things like that."

Although Hylas had planned to leave the talking entirely up to Zo, he had thought of something potentially useful to say.

"Do you … do you think he's lying to you when he says he doesn't really like it?" he ventured.

"No. I believe him. I do. I just don't know, sometimes, what he's getting from me, if it's enough. You know, because I've got to *keep* him. I was always proud to have a patron, but now Mistress is going on about how we all *have* to have one, and I've got worried. If this house loses any more reputation, is he going to decide it isn't worth coming to see me? If I was a girl, I'd try to get pregnant. Shit. I wish I could do that. Then even if he left me or died, I'd have a kid, like Theano does."

"Chrestos," Zo cut him off, "try to come back down to earth. You're worried. Of course. This thing with Mistress has got us all worried."

"I … love him."

Zo nodded. "Yeah. You've known that for a long time."

"Yeah. And I want him to be happy. If he wants to leave because of whatever—I'm gonna let him go. I'd hate it, but … " He swiped at his nose; he had started to cry. "And if he wanted to take me away because this place has … because he thinks this place has gone to shit—I think … I'm pretty sure … I'd go."

"You definitely should, Chrestos," said Zo.

Hylas nodded encouragingly.

"You don't owe the Red Balconies anything," Zo went on. "We're your friends, and that won't change, but the place is just a place."

"Yeah, but I love it here. I don't want to leave. What would I do? Just sit in Themi's house waiting for him while he's away at sea? I'm sure as shit not going to sea with him.

Themi wouldn't want me to, but even if he did … " He shook himself slightly. "Speaking of patrons—how's it going with Timon, Zo?"

"Fine," Zo said crisply.

It was something he and Hylas never talked about, though Hylas had assumed Zo discussed the progress of the affair—did you call it an affair?—with the other companions. He had a fleeting thought of getting up and finding an excuse to leave so that Zo and Chrestos could talk now. But actually it had been pretty clear that Zo had nothing more to say.

It was clear to Chrestos, too, and he was offended.

"Is that it? I just told you a big secret about my patron— seriously, if that ever got out, he'd be really embarrassed. Are you not going to reciprocate even a little bit?"

Zo shrugged, in a way that Hylas thought he would have found maddening if he had been Chrestos. "Timon's not my patron yet. That's … all there is to say."

"He shouldn't have to be embarrassed," Hylas blurted, to change the subject. "Themistokles. He … it's sad, that he would be embarrassed. Just because he doesn't want sex? That's not a bad way to be. It doesn't hurt anyone."

"Yeah?" Chrestos looked at him. "Everybody thinks you're probably that way yourself. All the girls think that."

"Chrestos, that's not … " Zo protested.

"I don't know," Hylas heard himself saying before he could think better of it. "I don't know if I am or not."

Chrestos gave him a sceptical look. "You don't know if you like sex or not."

Hylas nodded.

"Well … you're on Tykanos, man. You should find out."

After a moment, all three of them laughed.

CHAPTER 12

IT WAS NEARING the end of the year when Zo finally decided he would have to let Timon into his bed. The man had said something very unsubtle about wanting to "sample the goods" before making a commitment. He knew very well what was going on.

He had also developed an irritating conviction that Zo was an innocent, or at least shy. That was perhaps only natural when Timon had been making his interest plain for weeks without receiving an enthusiastic response, but it was still annoying. The man had lived most of his life on Tykanos; he knew how companions operated. Yet he was so convinced that he must be an exception to the rule that the only explanation for Zo keeping him at arm's length was that Zo was a shy flower?

Zo couldn't really complain to anyone about it. Chrestos might have been sympathetic, but Zo had probably burned his bridges with Chrestos by failing to confide in him earlier. The women were all struggling to find someone as interested in them as Timon was in Zo, and the stakes were higher for them—letting a man into their beds meant risking pregnancy. Zo couldn't ask them to listen to his complaints.

Hylas would have listened and offered sympathy. He might even have had something helpful to say, if Zo had asked for advice. But Zo couldn't bring himself to talk to Hylas about Timon. When he was with Hylas, he tried to pretend Timon didn't exist. And Hylas had had something to do with bringing Timon to the Red Balconies in the first place; Zo didn't want to seem ungrateful.

So on the 31st of Tenth Month, the last day of the Pseuchaian year, Zo let Timon linger while his other guests took their leave, until it was just the two of them alone in his room.

Timon raised his wine cup and drained it. He looked at Zo, his eyes dark in the lamplight.

"Is tonight the night that my skittish beauty finally relents?" he murmured.

Zo raised his eyebrows and blinked at him as though he might not have heard or understood what that meant. He was not going to encourage this kind of thing. But he moved closer to Timon on the divan—it was a nice, firmly cushioned one that Hylas had brought home for him from the governor's mansion, where it was being discarded in a redecoration—and plucked the empty wine cup from Timon's hand to set it on the table.

He should let the man make the first move; clearly he was the sort who would want to. Would he lean in for a kiss, or slide his hand onto Zo's thigh as he had tried to do more than once before?

He toyed with a strand of Zo's hair. So far, so good.

"You know I am a weapons merchant," he said.

"Mm."

"I have one very special spear I have been … *burning* to show you."

Zo laughed. He couldn't help it. He knew he wasn't supposed to; that hadn't been uttered in a tone that invited laughter. He tried to turn the laugh into a nervous giggle, didn't think he was particularly successful.

"You may have heard that I'm a ladies' man." Timon frowned slightly. "I have that reputation, I know. But not to worry. I know my way around the rear of a pretty youth."

"Just that part?" He would not laugh again. Angels of the Almighty, let him not laugh again.

Timon himself was still entirely serious. "I mean I've bedded a few boys in my time. Though they have to be quite special to pique my interest."

"I'm choosy myself."

Timon's frown deepened, and he shifted on the divan. "Erm … on the whole, I think it will be better if you don't talk back."

"Oh?"

"You're quite good at it, but I don't feel it will help my prowess."

"Oh."

"Are we clear, then?"

"Yes, sir, absolutely."

And indeed it *was* clear. Timon wanted playacting; or rather, he really wanted a squirming, reluctant boy, but he'd realized, having at least half a brain, that Zo wasn't that, and instead wanted him to pretend to be. And Zo, who'd never been squirming or reluctant even when he had been a boy, wanted to throw up.

He ducked his head so that his hair fell like a curtain, half-hiding his face. He could do playacting, of course. He did it all the time, had acted one part or another most of his life, often under much more challenging circumstances. He could do it, but he didn't want to. He wanted a night of enjoyable sex, and he should have known before now that he wasn't going to get it.

Timon moved toward him on the divan. He had soft hands, white and well-manicured. One of them slid under

Zo's hair and cupped his face, and he pulled Zo toward himself to kiss him. Zo came pliantly and allowed himself to be kissed. Some people liked it like this, he reminded himself: letting the other person take charge, feigning passivity. Maybe it would turn out that he liked it too.

"That's a good boy," Timon murmured when he had taken his tongue out of Zo's mouth finally. He was a terrible kisser. "Is it strange, kissing a man with a beard?"

"Oh, no, sir." Did Timon think he was the only bearded man on the island? And where did he imagine Zo was from, that he would find beards a novelty?

Timon was giving him an exasperated look.

"Well, perhaps a little," Zo simpered.

Timon's thumb toyed with Zo's lower lip. "You will grow used to it. Now, then. It is past time I delved under these trappings"—He plucked at the front of Zo's robe—"and plundered the treasure within."

Zo liked stripping bare for his lovers. He liked feeling their gaze on him in the lamplight and the slide of skin against skin in gratuitous cuddling when he convinced them to get naked too. It was a cold night, but the room was warmed by a brazier, and there were blankets piled generously on the bed.

Timon didn't even take off all of Zo's clothes. He undid a couple of buttons on Zo's robe and stuck his hand in, fumbling with Zo's undershirt—it was cold, he was wearing layers—to tweak a nipple perfunctorily, acting as if he were committing the ravishment of the century. He delivered some more unpleasant kisses. Zo was getting a crick in his neck from the way Timon bent his head back.

After that, Timon hitched up his own mantle and tunic, twitched aside his loincloth, and persisted in describing his cock as a spear. Zo was desperate for him to shut up. He'd never felt less aroused when actually in the lead-up to making love.

"You see how it strains to plunge into your dainty hole?" Timon was saying. "Down, boy!" He gave his cock an open-handed slap that made it bounce. "This beauty is no bitch to be mounted without preliminaries."

Maybe the earth would open up and swallow him, Zo thought wistfully. Maybe there would be an earthquake, and the island would subside under the sea. Maybe Hylas would come home tipsy and open the wrong door by accident. God, that would be nice. And wasn't all that far-fetched.

Timon's idea of preliminaries consisted of pulling Zo's trousers down—not all the way off, just down—positioning him on his knees on the cold floor, bent over the table, and poking a licked finger in his ass. He really did only know his way around a man's rear, apparently; he didn't touch Zo's cock, and only commented disapprovingly on his pubic hair. "I prefer my boys bare in that region," he said, to which Zo made no reply.

Zo had never found Planting the Rose, as it was called in the Zashian love manuals, did anything for him, but he was used to exaggerating signs of pleasure for the sake of lovers who really craved it. That in itself could be enjoyable, so in the end he usually had fun, even if he didn't climax. He didn't think Timon wanted him to pretend to enjoy himself. He clenched his muscles to give Timon the satisfaction of purring about how tight he was, and made breathy gasps that corresponded to nothing in particular.

"There's oil on my dressing table," he said, when he felt Timon change position behind him and begin to withdraw his finger.

"Shh-shh, my lovely. Your capacious hole will be able to accommodate even such girth as mine, have no fear."

Timon did, in fact, have a large cock, and Zo was absolutely not taking it without oil. He pushed himself up on his hands and looked over his shoulder.

"Sorry, but we do need the oil. I'll get it, shall I?"

Timon, who had his clothing bunched up in one hand and his cock in the other, glared at him for a moment as if not quite comprehending.

"No," he said finally, tugging down his mantle and struggling to his feet. "You stay where you are. Demanding little whore."

He stormed over to Zo's dressing table, now half-hidden by the screen Hylas had put up, knocked several things over, and returned, glowering, with the flask of oil. He made a mess with it, grunting and muttering about being put off his stride and how much he hated having greasy hands.

The actual fuck would have been an anticlimax if Zo had had any hopes for it. Timon had stamina but no technique. If Zo had been less uncomfortable, he thought he would probably have fallen asleep. Instead he put on a show with moans and protests—"too much," "too big," and so on. It wasn't any of those things; it was just boring and taking too long. Timon panted and growled and slapped Zo's flank and muttered disjointed nonsense—mercifully he wasn't able to keep talking coherently while he fucked.

Once Timon had come, he was restored to a good humour, the debacle with the oil largely forgotten. He hauled Zo up from the table and draped him prone on the divan, with his trousers still around his ankles, saying with obvious satisfaction that he looked "well used." As Zo had expected, he didn't stay. If he'd noticed that at no point during his lovemaking had Zo been aroused, he didn't comment on it. Probably that was how he liked it.

When he was gone, Zo sat up on the divan, rubbing his stiff neck, and kicked off his trousers. He retrieved his new crutch from the hiding place he and Hylas had found for it—close at hand but not obvious to his guests—and took down his lamp from its stand. It was late, but he very much wanted a bath.

"It's the last night of the year, Hylas," Loukianos announced, slapping Hylas on the shoulder. "We'll mark the funeral of the old year in the Sasian style, by drinking until the wee hours. Mind you, the Sasian calendar doesn't end the year here, but what odds?"

"When do the Sasians celebrate the new year?" Hylas asked. *And do they give gifts?* was going to be his next question. He was still regretting his lost opportunity at Dendreia.

"Spring some time?" said Loukianos vaguely. "We're going to the Peacock tonight."

An evening at the Peacock, in Hylas's opinion, was a better evening than one spent at the Bower or the Amber Lily. There would be good food and drink, some form of entertainment, and he might get the opportunity to say hello to Mutari. He always tried to pass on greetings to her from Theano and the others at the Red Balconies when he could.

Unfortunately, going to the Peacock did mean that Pantaleon, the most annoying of the governor's set, would be with them. He never came to the Bower of Suos and had apparently been banned from the Amber Lily.

No one else seemed to like Pantaleon any better than Hylas, and they were more successful in avoiding him, so that it ended up being Hylas whom he followed, talking loudly, into Mutari's sitting room. She was holding court there, as she did, arranged like a temple idol on her divan at one end of the room, with her guests seated around her and her patron, the quartermaster from the fort, in pride of place beside her. She waved Hylas in with a smile, and he picked his way through the crowd to a vacant cushion. Pantaleon blundered in behind him.

"How are my friends at the Red Balconies?" Mutari inquired.

"Very well," said Hylas, because this was a public inquiry,

Mutari doing her part to help rebuild the reputation of her friends' house.

Later, if they had an opportunity to talk privately, he could tell her how everyone was really doing, the latest in the battle between Mistress Aula and Taris over the headscarf, how Elpis had invented a new kind of cake without any flour, after a barrel that Aula had bought at a discount had turned out to be full of weevils.

"You have friends at the Red Balconies?" said one of Mutari's guests, as if playing along. Perhaps Mutari had put him up to it. "I didn't know that old house was still open."

"Oh, indeed it is," said the quartermaster. "I have many fond memories of the Red Balconies."

"We ought to go back some time," said someone else.

"It's a dump," said Pantaleon, loudly.

Everyone looked at him, though not with expressions which suggested they wanted to hear what he had to say next. That never seemed to bother him.

"They've only got a handful of girls," he went on, "and they're the worst shrews you can imagine. Bossy, standoffish, hardly even pretty—I don't know what any of them are doing as companions, they'd be better off as fishwives, I tell you."

"Now that you mention it," someone else muttered, "I did hear … "

And then it clicked in Hylas's mind. The name Pantaleon. That was where he'd heard it before.

"You used to live there, didn't you?" he cried, louder than necessary.

"What?" said Mutari, leaning forward with a look of interest, instantly drawing all eyes in the room back to Pantaleon and Hylas.

"You were their tenant," Hylas pursued. "You rented a room from them. They still talk about you."

Pantaleon huffed. "I doubt that. They were glad enough to get rid of me. Absolute harpies."

"No, they do talk about you—they do talk about him," Hylas addressed Mutari and by extension the rest of the room, "because he made off with their furniture when he left."

"He didn't!" Mutari exclaimed. "You didn't, did you?"

Pantaleon opened and shut his mouth like a fish. "Well, they were charging me too much rent. And they failed to give proper notice. My uncle is a jurist. I know my rights."

"I'm a jurist myself," said another guest. "Your rights as a tenant don't entitle you to take your landlord's furnishings, unless both parties have appeared in court and a judgement …"

"What else did he do?" the quartermaster asked. "Something tells me that's not the extent of the gossip."

"I don't want to repeat slander," Hylas said demurely, looking at Pantaleon.

Pantaleon stuck his chin out. "Too right! What else do they claim I did?"

"Kept trying to use their bath? But I don't—I mean, I can't really believe you'd do that."

"They're a bunch of frigid prudes! It was *one time*. Well, two times if you count—but it's a brazen lie to say I *kept* trying."

Mutari's guests that evening were mostly older men, friends of the quartermaster, and very gentlemanly. There was a lot of harrumphing, several people talked sententiously about the respect due to companions, and someone referred to the Red Balconies as a "venerable institution." All in all, Hylas felt it was a good evening's work.

Pantaleon slunk away after that, which made Hylas feel he should stay, although he had been thinking of making it an early night. So he lounged in Mutari's comfortable sitting room, drinking her wine and listening to her guests discuss politics and trade and the weather in Pheme, which everyone agreed was not as good as the weather on Tykanos. Before he knew it, the night was well worn, and even some of the regular guests were beginning to get up and head home.

Hylas made his own farewells, to Mutari and the quartermaster and a couple of guests she had introduced him to, and went looking for the governor. It was slightly strange that he hadn't seen Loukianos since their arrival. Usually, if they ended up in different parts of the house, Loukianos would come to check on Hylas at some point in the evening. But perhaps he didn't feel he needed to do that anymore, now that Hylas was more comfortable in the tea houses. Hylas smiled at the thought. Still, he didn't think the governor would have gone home without telling him.

And indeed he hadn't. Hylas found him, after wandering through the house, sitting in a corner of one half-deserted room, next to a very young female companion.

"Loukianos, I'm about to head out," Hylas called from halfway across the room.

The governor looked up. His eyes looked unfocussed, his features slack. He was dead drunk. Hylas had never seen him like this.

"Oh, sir, are you his friend?" asked the young companion, starting up from the cushion beside Loukianos. "Hylas?"

Hylas came across the room to Loukianos's corner. "Yes, I'm Hylas. Does he—is he all right? Loukianos? Are you all right?"

"He wouldn't let me hire him a chair until you returned," the girl said miserably. "But now perhaps … "

"It's been two years," Loukianos mumbled. "Two years to the day." He looked up at Hylas. "Two years since Hippolytos died."

"Do you know who that was?" the young companion asked. "He's mentioned him several times."

"He was your lover, wasn't he?" said Hylas.

"He went to sea and never came back," said Loukianos. "So many of them do, it's commonplace. And yet, when it

122

happens to you … " He made a hopeless gesture. "Now here I am, two years later. And here you are, Hylas, and you, Lara."

"Lada," the companion whispered.

"Pleased to meet you," Hylas murmured back, automatically.

He wasn't sure what to do about Loukianos. Drag him home, as he would have done with a labourer whom he found drunk outside a wine shop? Or let him talk, because he was after all the governor?

"There are so many things that I regret," Loukianos went on.

Let him talk, Hylas decided. If he'd needed to get this drunk in order to say what he wanted to say, best not to let that effort go to waste. Hylas sat on the cushion beside Loukianos. Lada dropped down on the other side, biting her lip. Loukianos gazed slowly at each of them in turn.

"Here I am," he said again. "And here you are. Just as … Isn't she beautiful, Hylas? Lara—isn't she beautiful?"

"Ab-absolutely." Hylas shot Lada an apologetic look.

"I can't do anything with a beautiful woman. Never have been able to. Pitiful, isn't it?"

Lada and Hylas made soothing noises.

"I was married once. Lovely young girl. Friend of the family. Thought I could hack it." He hung his head. "I divorced her, in the end, for her own sake. She's better off without me. It might have ruined my career—thought it would—but I couldn't keep her trapped like that."

"That was caring of you, sir," said Lada.

"Then I came here and met Hippolytos, and it was all different. He wasn't like me. Girls, men—" Loukianos threw back his head suddenly and laughed aloud. Lada and Hylas both started. "He could take pleasure with anyone. By the gods, how I loved him."

Hylas put a hand on the governor's shoulder. "I think it's

good to remember that, sir. Even if it is painful—even though *of course* it is painful." He was starting to tear up himself.

Loukianos looked down at Hylas's hand, then up into Hylas's face. Some thought was clearly forming, slowly, in his mind, but Hylas could not guess what it was.

Loukianos reached suddenly for Lada's hand, and removing Hylas's hand from his shoulder, brought the two of them clumsily together.

"Take Lara to bed, Hylas."

"What?" Hylas yelped.

Lada had frozen, eyes wide like a deer facing a hunter.

"She's a beautiful girl. Take her to bed. I'll just watch. You won't even know I'm there."

"Governor Loukianos, sir … " Lada began wretchedly. "I … "

"Let go of us, please," said Hylas, trying to withdraw his hand without violence. But Loukianos was squeezing his wrist fervently.

"I always wanted to ask Hippolytos for this, but I never had the courage. I know, I know it's perversion, I should be ashamed … "

"Oh, no, sir," Lada began, "it's just … "

"Don't be ashamed," said Hylas, finding firm ground now, to his relief. "You want what you want. And you can have it here—it's Tykanos. Makes—makes Boukos look like a jurist's funeral, I—I've heard. But Loukianos, Lada is a companion, and the companions of Tykanos are accomplished entertainers who deserve our respect." He was quoting one of Mutari's guests, word for word. "You cannot tell her to go to bed with a man she doesn't even know."

"But you're wonderful!" Loukianos cried indignantly.

"I—that's very kind of you, sir, but—"

"He saved a town from a volcano, you know," Loukianos informed Lada.

"No, I—it wasn't a—"

"And you can see for yourself how considerate he is. He's not as handsome as Hippolytos, but nobody is, and if you like Ariatan looks, you can't deny he has a fine physique."

"Loukianos!" Hylas withdrew his hand, forcefully, and got to his feet. "I'm going to send for a chair to take you home."

"Oh, I can do that," said Lada, jumping up too. "Please, let me do that."

"Absolutely. Go ahead. And sorry about—all this. You seem lovely—"

"So do you, sir. Good—good luck with everything."

"Let's get up now, Loukianos," said Hylas, crouching to look the governor in the eye.

"I don't feel altogether well," said Loukianos thoughtfully.

Then he leaned forward and vomited directly onto Hylas's chest.

Hylas cleaned himself up and was able to borrow a fresh tunic to wear home, but he still arrived back at the Red Balconies feeling like he needed a bath. When he came into the deserted courtyard, he was greeted by the sound of water splashing in the newly restored fountain. He filled a bucket and headed for the men's bath.

There was a lamp lit in the outer room of the bath, and the inner door was closed. Yawning, Hylas set down his bucket and stripped off his borrowed tunic. He opened the door.

The inner room of the bath was lit only by a taper burning in a socket on the wall, but the air was warm and steamy. Zo was sitting on a low stool in the shadows. He looked up at Hylas, dark eyes wide.

He was an elegant shape in the warm semi-darkness, long limbs bare and wet, black hair falling softly over his shoulder. He was sitting with his forearms on his knees, holding a dripping sponge that he had been using to wash himself from the basin of warm water in front of him. He must have built a fire in the masonry stove in the corner to warm the water and put another basin on the stove to produce steam.

He smiled. "Hello, Hylas. I didn't expect to see you."

"I … didn't expect to see you."

Of course he should have realized, from the lit lamp and closed door, that there was someone in the bath, but he hadn't. He never would have opened the door if he had thought Zo was inside. Zo was from one of those places where people didn't bathe communally. He deserved his privacy.

And yet Hylas went on standing there, not retreating and shutting the door, because Zo was looking at him with … appreciation?

It was not right. He was middle-aged. Zo was young and beautiful—so, so beautiful, with that flawless skin and supple, gently curvaceous frame—and it was not right for Hylas to stand there, nearly naked, under Zo's scrutiny, and feel suddenly, absurdly desirable.

"I shouldn't let the steam out," Hylas said, reaching for the door handle.

"Yes, but—stay on this side of it?"

"I will."

He shut the door and came to sit on the built-in bench opposite Zo, mimicking Zo's posture with his arms on his knees. Zo dipped his sponge in the water and squeezed it out.

"You won't believe the night I had, Hylas."

"No? Was it good?"

"*So* bad."

"Did you get thrown up on, though?"

Zo grinned. "Oh, your evening was good too, was it?"

126

"Well, parts of it were all right."

"But did you have to pretend to be a ravished innocent for a man who refers to his cock as a 'lustful spear'?"

"Oh, no!" He hadn't thought about why Zo would be bathing in the middle of the night, but presumably—well, it would be messy, and if you hadn't enjoyed it … "Are you all right?" He didn't know if it was the right question, but it was the one that came to mind.

Zo's smile softened. "I'm fine. Timon's not patron material, though. He doesn't really like men. I think he likes the idea of fucking a boy every so often for variety, or to show his range or something. I don't see him really becoming attached. Which is a relief, because Angels of the Almighty, is he rubbish in bed. And has a bit of a mean streak, actually, which I wouldn't like to explore further."

"I'm sorry," said Hylas with feeling.

"You mean because you sent him here? Don't worry, you weren't to know."

"I … I didn't send him here. He—wouldn't have been my choice for you. I've never liked him."

"Oh! I thought … because you said you'd look for a rich man for me, and then he showed up, and he knew you—and was obviously trying to make you jealous, which was … " Zo made a face. "Pretty tacky, really."

"I guess I must have given him the idea, because I suggested the Red Balconies one night. But I didn't mean for him to come by himself. I was hoping the whole group would come. I wanted you to meet the governor."

"The *governor*? Hylas! I'm not that ambitious."

"I know, but the two of you could talk about gardening. And if you could be happy together—you're both my friends. I'd like to see that."

Zo was silent for a long moment. "Well," he said finally. "Is it too late?"

"It might be. He's the one who threw up on me tonight.

He was very drunk. If he remembers any of what he said, he may not want to look me in the eye ever again." Hylas smiled. "But I'll see."

Hylas stood up and scooped water from his own bucket to splash over his chest. The chill was bracing in the warm room.

"You didn't warm that up!" Zo yelped.

"I'm Ariatan. 'Warm baths are for weaklings.'"

He struck a virile pose, and Zo threw his wet sponge at him. It missed. Hylas picked it up, wrung it out, and tossed it gently back.

Then he turned away so Zo could finish his bath, so he wouldn't see the unfolding of those graceful limbs as Zo stood, his beautiful body fully displayed. If Zo wanted to look at him while he stripped off his loincloth and scrubbed himself ... If Zo wanted to look at *him*? It was ridiculous.

And yet he could almost feel Zo's gaze travelling over his skin. Did Zo like his height and his square shoulders? His freckles? He had met a girl once who'd liked the freckles, and an old woman had once told him in the street that he had a nice ass—though she had probably not been quite sane.

"I'll wait outside the door until you're done," he said without turning around, "and help you put out the fire and close up the bath."

CHAPTER 13

"Pani and Menthe say they have a surprise for everyone, and we've all got to come to the best winter sitting room," Chrestos said, hanging off the doorframe to look into Zo's room. "Where's Aqueduct Man? I knocked on his door, but there was no answer."

"He's out doing aqueduct things—he doesn't actually work here, you know."

"Oh. I just got used to him being around most of the time. He's like a member of the family, you know?"

"All right, I'll be there in a minute. Tell them, will you?"

Pani and Menthe had been busy with something for weeks that they had been trying to keep secret from Mistress Aula. Zo had no inkling of what it was, though he thought Theano and Taris were in on the secret and had been helping to keep it quiet.

He had breakfasted with Hylas that morning as usual, the part of his day that he wouldn't have missed for worlds, no matter how tired he was. They had talked as usual, though Zo had been distracted by picturing Hylas's strong, straight back and trim ass. He wondered what Hylas had been thinking about.

Zo made his way upstairs to the best winter sitting room. The rest of the household, save Mistress Aula, was gathered in the gallery outside the door, wrapped in shawls and looking sleepy—except for Menthe and Pani, who were holding hands and looked nervously excited.

"What *is* it?" Chrestos groaned. "I'm dying to know!"

"You'll find out when Mistress gets here," said Pani.

"Oh, I hope she likes it," said Menthe.

Mistress Aula came up the stairs a few minutes later, enveloped in a patterned red mantle. She looked suspicious.

"What's going on?"

"We have a surprise for you, Mistress," said Pani. Zo noticed that she moved to let go of Menthe's hand, but Menthe held on.

"Come inside and see," Menthe said.

She opened the door to the sitting room, and she and Pani stepped inside. The rest of the group held back to let Mistress Aula follow them. She stopped just inside the door and gasped.

"Who did this? Who did you get? It must have cost a fortune!"

"We did it ourselves," Pani said. "Menthe and I."

What they'd done, Zo saw when he finally got to look in through the doorway, was painted frescoes in the best winter sitting room, all over one wall and part of another. Frescoes of garden scenes with birds in the trees, a favourite decorative scheme of Mistress Aula's, and domed buildings in the distance suggestive of Zash. It was breathtaking. You hardly noticed now that the cushions were threadbare and the floor needed waxing.

"Pani did all the drawing," Menthe was explaining, "and I helped put in the colours. We're not finished—"

"But we thought the guests would like to watch us work," Pani completed her sentence.

"We needed to do this much to perfect our technique before we showed it to you," Menthe went on.

"But if you like it, we can do other rooms in the house, too."

Mistress Aula had begun to cry. "It's so perfect. No one in town has anything like this. It will—it will set us apart. And I thought none of you liked me!"

There was an awkward silence. Menthe was the one who broke it.

"We don't want the Red Balconies to fail, Mistress. We … "

"It's our home," said Pani. "We wanted to do what we can to help."

"It was a triumph," said Taris, hugging Menthe, after Mistress had gone.

"I didn't know you could do frescoes," said Chrestos. "I mean, I knew you draw, Pani, and you're both good with colours in your weaving and that, but painting frescoes?"

"We had to learn some techniques. Do you remember that man Pamphilos who was our guest a bunch of times back in Eighth Month? He's a fresco painter from Boukos who's here for the winter, doing work at someone's house on the mountain. He agreed to teach us for free drinks and food. It was very kind of him."

"We're hoping Mistress won't make us go after garlands from men if we can do something else to help the house," Pani explained. "We don't want patrons."

"Your hearts are already bestowed," said Taris with a romantic sigh.

"What?" said Chrestos, looking around as though he'd missed something. "On who?"

"On each other, you giant dimwit." Taris rolled her eyes.

That made sense, and Zo felt rather a giant dimwit himself for not having realized it. He couldn't wait to tell Hylas and find out if he had.

As luck would have it, and much to Mistress Aula's delight, they were able to show off the frescoes that afternoon, and without any expenditure on lamp oil. A group of guests arrived during tea hours, something that hadn't been happening much recently.

They were a random assortment that worked surprisingly well together, a pleasing thing when it happened. There were a couple of regulars who had stopped coming some time ago, a pair of jurists who knew the Red Balconies only by reputation and said they had heard it talked about favourably the other night, and a young Zashian, bearded and trousered and looking fresh from Suna, a stranger to the Red Balconies and to Tykanos tea houses in general.

They were all enchanted by Pani and Menthe's frescoes. The jurists and the regulars loved the idea of watching them prepare the next section of the composition. The Zashian gravitated rather shyly toward Zo and Taris.

"You must be from the Parkan," he said to Zo, speaking in a tentative mixture of Zashian and Pseuchaian, as if unsure which language Zo would understand best.

"I am," said Zo in Zashian. "My name is Temar."

The Zashian beamed gratefully, his smile white in his dark beard.

"And you," he addressed Taris even more shyly, "are from my mother's homeland, I can tell by the way you wrap your headscarf."

"Your mother is from Shavadi?" said Taris delightedly. "I so rarely meet anyone from there. I was not born in Shavadi, but my master moved there from Seleos when I was a little girl. I served in the household of a Shavad mountain lord for a while."

"Truly? My mother told me stories of them when I was a boy! What are they really like?"

Zo, who had heard stories of the mountain lords of Shavadi when he was a boy too, listened with interest as Taris described her former life. Their Zashian guest already seemed perfectly at ease.

"What name did you give Nahaz?" Taris asked later, after the early guests had left. "Temar? Is that your real name?"

"Oh. No, but it's a typical Parkan name, and 'Zo' isn't." He shrugged. "I thought it would confuse him if I didn't have a Parkan name." He'd put on a slight Parkan accent when speaking Zashian to Nahaz, too, but Taris didn't seem to have noticed that.

She frowned. "Well, he seemed to have a good time, so he may come back. You'd be better off giving him your real name then."

"He'll think I *did* give him my real name, and that Zo is a nickname. This isn't my first chariot race, you know."

That seemed to satisfy her, and she laughed and let the topic drop.

Hylas did not expect to see Loukianos at the government office that day. But he came in, late in the afternoon, looking grey-faced and worse for wear. He shuffled some documents about and talked to a few people before finally coming over to Hylas's desk.

"Hylas," he said grimly. He leaned against the desk, arms folded.

Hylas held his breath. Clearly the governor remembered what had gone on the night before and was embarrassed by it. And a man in his position could easily make such a problem go away. Dismissing Hylas would be simple—logical, even, with the aqueduct project stalled and perhaps moribund.

Of course he didn't want to be dismissed, but equally he found he didn't want to see Loukianos abuse his power in that way. It would be unworthy of him.

"I have to apologize for last night," Loukianos said, and Hylas breathed again.

"It's all right, sir," he said easily.

"No, no, it isn't. I can only imagine what you must think of me."

There were other people in the office, though none very near them.

"I think you were upset and grieving, and I'd never hold that against you. As … as for the other … " He lowered his voice further. "You know, it's not really anything I know much about, but I'm sure you can make it happen. Not—not with me, that wouldn't work, and probably not with that young woman at the Peacock, but I daresay there are people on the island who would quite like the idea."

Loukianos had been staring fixedly down at the desk, but now he looked up at Hylas. "You're probably right. It is Tykanos, after all."

"Exactly what I was thinking."

But in fact, when he thought about it more, after Loukianos went off to another part of the office to speak to someone, he thought that Tykanos wasn't quite what everyone made it out to be. It was more complex, more difficult to grasp—like a person with many sides to their character.

The garden door rattled open briefly and shut again, a breath of cold air wafting over the bed, and Hylas was in the room; Zo could feel his presence even if he wouldn't open his eyes.

"Zo, it's mid-morning. You should get up."

"I'm tired," Zo snarled from the depths of his pillow.

A pause. Then Hylas's voice again, gentle and sympathetic but somehow also implacable: "I know. But you told me that lying in bed all day doesn't help and that you often feel better when you get up. So I've come to remind you that you should try that."

"I don't want to."

"I know. I'm here to help, though. What if I get you some fresh tea?"

"Mph." Zo finally opened his eyes and peered at the chair beside his bed. There was the tray which Hylas must have left earlier, the tea bowl full but obviously quite cold by now. "Was I awake when you came earlier?"

"I thought you were, but perhaps not."

"Fresh tea would be nice."

Very briefly, Hylas touched his shoulder—just the slightest tap of his fingers through the blanket.

"I'll be right back." Another pause. "Is it all right if I come in through your front door, from the hall?"

"Why wouldn't it be?"

"Um, I don't know. Sorry. Never mind."

Zo thought about that while Hylas was gone, instead of falling back to sleep as he'd planned. Maybe Hylas had been afraid someone would see him going into Zo's room if he went in from the hall? It was more or less a secret that they visited each other so much. They were never together outside their corner of the house.

He closed his eyes but wasn't asleep when Hylas returned. He pushed himself up onto one elbow in bed to show his intention of following Hylas's advice.

"Sorry I took so long," Hylas said, setting the fresh pot of tea on the tray.

He picked up the bowl of cold tea and drained it in a couple of gulps instead of tossing it out. Zo winced, but

Hylas didn't seem to notice that. He refilled the bowl from the pot and offered it to Zo.

"Elpis was telling me all about Pani and Menthe's frescoes."

"Mm." Zo sat up, cradling the warm bowl. "It's the talk of the house. Who's Elpis?"

Hylas had taken a seat on the floor by Zo's bed. "The cook."

"Isn't the cook a man? Tio, Timo-something?"

"Timoto. He's the night cook. Elpis is the day cook."

"Oh. Shocking that I didn't know that, isn't it?"

"A little bit."

"You're friends with the kitchen staff. I remember you saying that, a long time ago, when I made a joke about how they must like you because they'd given you the good tea."

"I spent many years with no friends and am making up for lost time."

Zo looked down at Hylas. His own life hadn't exactly been full of friendship before he came to this place—and then he'd spent most of this year sulking in his room, ignoring the friends he did have because it was too much work to try to make them understand his suffering. And even then, to befriend the kitchen staff—that, he realized with shame, would never have occurred to him.

"I know you said you lost your status in your homeland. Do you think of yourself as a commoner?"

"Absolutely. That surprises you?"

"Well. Yes. It sounded unjust, the way you were treated by your people. I guess I'd imagined you would rebel against that in your heart, if nowhere else."

"I do think it unjust now, but for most of my life I haven't. And I wouldn't want that status back, not with what it means in Ariata. Though … I have started using my old surname again, which I'm not at all entitled to do." He shrugged. "That doesn't make any sense, does it? It was that business with the dam at Koilas. I was starting to be … well, talked about, and I felt I needed a double name—most people who are in the public eye have two names. I could have invented one, I guess, but I liked my actual family name."

"What is it?"

"My surname? Mnemotios."

"Muh-neh … "

"Mnemotios."

"Neh-moh … Mneh?"

"Yeah. Mneh. Motios."

"That's a tongue-twister."

"Don't be silly. You're an accomplished young man. You don't have any difficulty pronouncing names."

"All right, all right. Mnemotios. Hylas Mnemotios. It is a nice name."

There was a knock at Zo's front door. Hylas started.

"Message for you!" came Mistress Aula's voice, sounding unusually cheerful.

Hylas was already on his feet. He slid the garden door open silently and slipped out as Zo was calling, "Coming!"

Zo swung his feet out of bed and went to the door, aggrieved that Hylas had been driven away so abruptly. Of course he wouldn't come back.

Mistress Aula didn't open the door herself before Zo got there, a mark of how pleased she evidently was with Zo at the moment. She was smiling when he opened the door, although the smile dimmed somewhat when she saw him.

"You look like a wreck."

"Thanks. I feel great, too."

"You need to take care of yourself."

"I do. I was. I had to get up to answer the door."

She sighed. "Right. Well, there's a message for you from Timon of Kos." She presented a tablet tied with a red ribbon.

"So, that's good. You, um, go rest or whatever you need to do."

He went to drop down onto his divan after she left, where he untied the ribbon around the tablet and flipped it open. It was just a note to tell him that Timon was busy and wouldn't be able to see him for a few days.

He hadn't finished his tea or touched the buns that Hylas had brought that morning, and now they were all the way on the other side of the screen at the far end of the room. He leaned his head back against the cushions and closed his eyes.

Another knock, this time Hylas's characteristic soft tap at the garden door. Zo's eyes popped open.

"Come!"

Hylas slipped back into the room.

"I thought you'd gone."

"I came back." He disappeared behind the screen by Zo's bed and reappeared with the tea tray.

"What would I do without you?" Zo sat up and accepted the bowl which Hylas had refilled with hot tea.

"Who's the message from? If—if it's my business. It's probably not my business."

"It's Timon. He's trying to play hard to get."

Hylas sat on the divan next to him, not very close. "Is that, um, how that's supposed to work?"

"No." Zo laughed. "It's a terrible gambit. I wish he'd just go away. I don't want to have to be the one to tell Mistress he's not a good prospect."

"I'll try to get the governor here before you have to," said Hylas, apparently serious.

"Is he still speaking to you? I thought we were afraid he was going to fire you for getting thrown up on."

"No, we're on good terms again, I think. He apologized."

"Good man. Well, invite him, then. By all means."

He was humouring Hylas, of course; he didn't really think the governor of Tykanos was likely to take up with him. A man like that would take a mistress from one of the big houses, someone with more status in the town than Zo would ever have. It would be foolhardy of him not to, no matter what his personal preferences might be.

"I have to go, I'm afraid," Hylas said, getting to his feet. "Do you need anything else?"

"No. I'm all right. I might go up and work with the girls for a while later."

"Good. I'm—I'm so glad you're doing that again. Well. I'm off."

Zo sketched a lazy wave and watched Hylas leave through the steam from his tea. He wondered if Hylas too had felt that it would have been natural for him to lean down and give Zo a parting kiss. No, probably not.

CHAPTER 14

FOR THE FIRST two weeks of the new year, Governor Loukianos did not go out to any of the tea houses. He didn't come to the government office much, either. Exactly what he was doing, in the dead of winter when he couldn't reasonably be gardening, Hylas didn't know. He wavered between feeling worried for the man, that he was perhaps sliding into a depression, and annoyed with him. He needed Loukianos to come to the Red Balconies to meet Zo, and he also needed him to do something, anything really, to help with the stalled aqueduct project.

Hylas was keeping himself busy working on the water infrastructure of the town. He had two teams now making repairs to the pipes, and they had restored water to all of the fountains that had been dry, although they had been obliged to shut off the supply to two of them, temporarily, because the volume of water currently entering the town wasn't sufficient to keep them all flowing.

In the second week of Turning Month, Mutari reported that she'd been able to arrange for Hylas and a couple of surveyors from the fort to visit the big island surreptitiously. They made it an overnight trip, camping in the forest near the site of the spring, and managed a thorough survey of the area that allowed Hylas, on his return to the government office, to begin planning the aqueduct in earnest. They were still, however, no closer to getting permission from Gylphos to build it.

Loukianos returned to the government office the day after Hylas got back from the big island, acting as if nothing had happened. Mostly. He asked Hylas how things had been at the Bower lately, and seemed surprised when Hylas said he didn't know because he hadn't been.

"Well, we must remedy that, then!" Loukianos declared heartily. "We must both make our triumphant return tonight."

In fact, Hylas had been enjoying the evenings at the Red Balconies. Some nights he burned incense and sat with the companions, watching Pani and Menthe work on their frescoes, listening to Zo play or sing or talk to his guests. But a couple of nights he had helped out Ahmos and the night cook, whom he had seen looking harried over one thing and another. He was not really a guest of the house, and it had seemed natural—felt better, even—to make himself useful than to sit around being entertained all the time.

"Mistress will make a joke about how she 'hopes you don't expect to be paid now'," Zo had said, gently imitating Aula's sharp tone. "And it won't sound like a joke, but it will be meant as one."

"I know," Hylas said. "I think I am beginning to understand how she is."

He would miss spending the evening at home with Zo and the others. But he didn't dread the prospect of returning to the Bower of Suos with the governor. Loukianos and his friends could be amusing in their way. And there was always the morning to look forward to.

"Actually," he told Zo the next day, "it was worse than I expected. I think they've been as gloomy at the Bower of

Suos the last two weeks as we were here at the end of the year. Not only has Loukianos abandoned them—and me, which they pretend to care about—"

"How implausible!"

"Yes, I know. And Timon of Kos hasn't been seen anywhere in weeks, either."

"Really?" Zo frowned. "He's written me a few times. I didn't mention it to you … "

"You don't have to tell me everything," Hylas said automatically. Certainly there were things, quite significant things about his own feelings, that he wasn't telling Zo.

"No. They weren't very interesting letters. A lot of stuff about how I'm torturing him. Not in a fun way. But I also assumed they weren't true. You know, that he was out at other tea houses amusing himself and not thinking about me all the time as he claimed." He made a face. "Clearly I'd better do something about that. It would be unprofessional not to."

Hylas didn't ask what he planned to do. It was none of his business.

It was a few days after the governor's triumphant return to the tea houses, and before Hylas had come up with a way to invite him to the Red Balconies, that Mutari proposed a trip to Tetum. Hylas at first didn't know what she was getting at, why she was mentioning it to him. Was it just because she thought it would be inconvenient for him if she went off to her homeland for an extended stay at this point? But there was nothing going on now; she'd already been tremendously helpful getting him to the big island with the surveyors, and he would have plenty to work on in her absence.

No, it turned out; she wondered if he wanted to come with her.

"I've become almost used to not making a fool of myself in every social situation," he told Zo the following morning, "but I certainly haven't forgotten how to do it. I didn't know what to say to her. 'Aren't you somebody's mistress? Are you allowed to invite me places?'"

"I mean, you could have said that." Zo sipped his tea. "She *is* somebody's mistress."

"'Will he kill me, though?' That's what I wanted to know. 'Will you have to hide me in your luggage?' Apparently not. Apparently he'd consider it a favour if I would go with her, as her escort. I barely know him, but she trusts me, and—he must trust her, so … I suppose I must also have a reputation of some sort that, er, helps."

It was a very strange thought. He'd never imagined there could be any advantage in having a public reputation as a man who had so little idea what to do with a woman that he could be trusted around other men's beautiful mistresses.

"Mm," said Zo diplomatically. "So, are you going to go?"

"Yes. The opportunity to visit Gylphos—there are lots of things in Tetum I'm interested to see, and to have a local guide, it's too good a chance to pass up. And of course she does think we may be able to make contacts that will help with the aqueduct."

Just when Hylas had begun to feel guilty for talking excitedly of a trip that Zo couldn't go on, Zo showed signs of being excited on Hylas's behalf, talking about the things he should look for in the market and the sights he should be sure to see—all of it based on hearsay, as Zo himself had never been to Tetum or any part of Gylphos. Hylas knew Zo was playing up his enthusiasm to be a good friend, and he insisted Zo tell him what he wanted brought back from the markets of Tetum as a present.

The trip to Tetum lasted two weeks, and he missed Zo the entire time. And yet he enjoyed himself thoroughly too. He bought Zo three presents: the sweets he had requested, a pair of earrings with bright blue enamel beads, and a fan of plaited reeds painted with a scene of water birds and a hippopotamus. He visited people with Mutari and had to do very little talking because most of them did not speak Pseuchaian, but everyone was very polite to him. They looked at famous buildings and ancient statuary, and a cousin of Mutari's gave him a tour of some farms that used interesting Gylphian irrigation techniques.

Another of Mutari's cousins kept trying to encourage him to talk to her teenage son, who did in fact speak Pseuchaian fairly well. Hylas assumed this was because the boy was interested in engineering, but this didn't seem to be the case. Eventually Mutari gave him a hint that the mother was probably trying to make a match between him and her son, having made assumptions about Hylas from the fact that he was Mutari's escort. Hylas realized that yes, the signs had been pointed that way fairly clearly. He also realized this was a story of his trip that he was not going to be able to tell Zo.

They had no luck finding anyone to talk to about the aqueduct. They learned that a new envoy to Tykanos had been sent by Suna, but after arriving in Tetum he had gone travelling, and no one knew exactly where he was. In some ways, business in Gylphos seemed to be done very similarly to business on Tykanos.

"Well," said Mutari, as they relaxed on the river boat on the first leg of their return journey, "at least we had a good time. I got to visit my cousins, you learned all that fascinating stuff about canals and bought some presents for your boyfriend … "

"He's not my boyfriend."

"Mm, I don't know about those earrings, then."

"No? Are they l-love token earrings, do you think?"

"A little bit. Just be prepared to have a conversation about your relationship if you give him those."

"Maybe I'll save them for his birthday. I don't want to make him uncomfortable."

He was looking forward so keenly to seeing Zo that it seemed almost wrong, as if he should have needed Zo's permission to think so much about him. He arrived back at the Red Balconies as the sun was setting, and just managed to catch Zo before he left his room to join the other companions upstairs. The way Zo beamed at him and shouted, "You're back!" was better than any of the sights of Tetum.

"I got you presents," he said, thrusting the parcel into Zo's hands as a substitute for what he suddenly wanted to do, which was hug Zo.

He'd completely forgotten to take the earrings out of the parcel, but Mutari had been wrong, or underestimated Zo, because there was no conversation about them. Zo gasped and exclaimed over them, took out the earrings he had been wearing to put them in, pinned back his hair to show them off, and looked at himself in his mirror.

"How did you know to pick these? I used to have a pair just like this when I was a boy. They were my favourite earrings."

"I just … thought they would suit you."

"I love them. And the fan, too." He picked it up, tracing his fingertips over the painted animals.

"I tried to pick the hippopotamus with the best expression," Hylas said.

"So how were things around here while I was gone?" Hylas asked Zo the following morning as they sat in his room.

Zo took a moment to think about that, under cover of sipping his tea. There were different ways he might have chosen to answer.

"Honestly, not too bad," he said finally. "Mistress has

been in a good temper—or, to do her justice, learning not to take it out on us when she isn't, I think. We have one new regular, a Zashian gentleman, Nahaz—did you ever meet him? Anyway, he's been coming pretty often, and he's a nice addition. Good manners—not court manners, just a solid middle-class type. He likes Taris because she reminds him of his mother, and she likes him because she likes reminding a man of his mother, I guess, and Mistress has decided she likes Taris's headscarf after all now, because it's part of the reminding-him-of-his-mother situation."

"Amazing. That's all working out, then."

"Mm. I have a new prospect myself," he added, reluctant to talk about it but feeling he should. "Or, well, a revival of an old prospect. One of my old regulars, who'd stopped coming for a while, is back with apologies. A man named Djosi. I had my eye on him as a patron a while back … around the time you moved in."

"Ah! That's good," said Hylas eagerly.

Zo found himself annoyed with the eagerness, and then felt childish. It wasn't as if he *wanted* Hylas to feel jealous.

"Well, we'll see. It came to nothing once before. On the opposite side of the ledger, Timon of Kos has been around a few times."

Hylas nodded. "Theano told me. She said he'd been bothering you. I, uh, didn't like to hear that."

Zo was glad he had mentioned it, then. He hadn't wanted to, but if Hylas had already known, he'd just have looked like he was keeping secrets.

"I knew you wouldn't. She didn't mean he's been doing anything sinister. Just making a fuss and sending letters and things. He's an unpleasant man, when you get to know him."

Hylas had a pained look on his face that Zo wanted desperately to smooth away somehow. "I should never have … I knew—I thought he was unpleasant myself."

"You didn't do anything, Hylas. You just talked about the Red Balconies around him, you didn't *tell* him to come here."

Hylas shook his head. "I'd heard him say things that revealed his character, and I should have told you instead of letting you pursue a-a liaison with him. What did he do?"

"Nothing. Hylas, don't blame yourself. I don't know what Theano told you. Timon came here a couple of times in an ill temper because he's had a quarrel with his wife."

"His *wife?*"

"Yes, Hylas. All these men are married."

"R-right. Loukianos isn't, so I suppose I forgot."

"Anyway, he came here. He followed me to my room one night and wasn't going to take 'no' for an answer, but I pretended to be feeling ill, and not in a pretty way … " It had been a transparent ruse, and he wasn't proud of it.

"Do you think he'll come back?"

"He may." He probably would.

"What can I do to help?"

"Oh, I don't know … " Zo prevaricated.

There was one obvious thing. It would likely make Timon go away for good. But he couldn't ask Hylas to pretend to be his lover, and it wasn't going to happen naturally. If he'd needed more proof of that, the gift of those expensive earrings, thrust into his hands unceremoniously with the cheap tourist items, had supplied that. Those earrings could have been a courtship present, but not given like that.

Hylas went back to the plans for the aqueduct, which he was able to complete now that he had visited the big island, and the work on repairing the pipes in town, which had ground to a halt for no good reason while he had been gone. He thought he might have a solution for the silting-up of the water intake at the new bath complex. The next couple of weeks were satisfyingly filled with real work; he would return to the Red Balconies in the evenings feeling that he had accomplished things.

Zo was busy in the evenings for a while with Djosi, who turned out to be the man Hylas had seen leaving Zo's room on one of his first nights at the Red Balconies. He was handsome and somewhat younger than Hylas, and he and Zo made an attractive pair, sitting together in the evenings. Hylas wished he could simply be happy for Zo without also feeling naggingly inferior whenever the man was around.

Mistress Aula clearly wasn't as pleased about Djosi as she had been about Timon of Kos—he wasn't nearly as rich—but she contented herself with oblique comments and pointed sighs. And then, as suddenly as he had reappeared, Djosi was gone again, this time seemingly for good.

"He offered a garland to a girl at the Amber Lily," Zo reported dispassionately when Hylas came home to find him lying face down on the divan. "I have to start all over again."

"I'm sorry," said Hylas. "Are you just … upset about that, or did you like him?"

Zo laughed as he hauled himself up to a sitting position. "Not tremendously, no. I certainly don't like his fickleness. What kind of man does that? He was throwing out *clear* hints he was going to ask to be my patron—was he giving her the same line the whole time, and then just flipped a coin to decide, or what? It's frustrating. I'm supposed to be good at this—why can't I get any man to … " He looked away.

"You will," said Hylas, feeling awkward. "You are good at this."

But for a moment he had thought, *He doesn't mean "any man"; he means me. Why can't he get me to … to what? To admit that I want him?* But what good would that do?

The following afternoon, when he had exhausted the

work that he could do for the day, Hylas got up from his desk and went into Loukianos's office. Loukianos sat up in his chair, clearly pretending he hadn't been about to doze off.

"Would you like to come to the Red Balconies this evening, sir?" Hylas asked.

"Eh? Oh, I suppose we've never been there yet, have we? And I said I was going to take you to all the tea houses. Of course, I don't think we've been to Myrrha's either, which is remiss of me ... "

"Well, yes, but the fact is I *have* been to the Red Balconies. I'm there all the time—I lodge there."

"Oh, is that a fact? I had no idea. Come to think of it, I did hear that they'd taken in lodgers. Wasn't Pantaleon their tenant for a while?"

"Mm. But I thought you might like to come with me tonight. The food is very good, and the music. You might find it ... a change of pace."

"A good thought, yes. A change of pace. I suppose I could. Is ... out of curiosity ... there used to be a companion there named Theano. Is she still around?"

"She is, yes."

"Mm. Just curious. Well, I suppose I could come," he said again. "What time did you think of going?"

"I thought to go now, actually. I don't have any more work to do here."

"Right." Loukianos scanned the surface of his desk, which held nothing in the way of excuses for lingering. "I'll join you, then."

Ought he to do this, after all? Did he want Loukianos to become Zo's patron? He, Hylas, was drawn to Zo, desired Zo himself. And there had been that look in Zo's eyes, that time in the bath, and that moment when he looked away, yesterday. Hylas held some interest for him that was not friendship. It wasn't madness to imagine ...

But Hylas could not be Zo's patron. He didn't even receive a steady salary from the governor, nor did he know how to ask for one.

So it *was* madness. Zo needed a patron, and Hylas could not fill that role, but Loukianos could. There was no use in thinking more about it.

The sun was beginning to get low in the sky when they arrived at the Red Balconies. Hylas was about to direct Loukianos toward Zo's room when they were met by Chrestos and Captain Themistokles, coming down the stairs from the gallery arm-in-arm.

"Governor Loukianos!" said the captain. "I didn't know you came here."

"I, er, haven't in some years. But my friend Hylas convinced me to come back."

"You've chosen a good day, sir," said Chrestos enthusiastically. "Two of our companions are just starting a new fresco in the south sitting room which you *must* see. It's the room at the far end of the gallery," he added to Hylas. "Everyone's up there already. Mistress Aula is away visiting a friend—she'll be sorry to have missed you, sir."

They were just lighting the lamps as Hylas and Loukianos entered. Pani was working on a wall full of delicate foliage, sketching in pencil, while Menthe sat chatting with the group of assembled guests. Zo was sitting on the far side of the room, and at the moment he seemed to have no guests attached to him. He saw Hylas and waved.

Hylas turned to Loukianos, who had frozen in the doorway, and drew him by the elbow into the room, thinking as he did what a strange reversal this was from the situation when he had first arrived on Tykanos only a few months ago.

"There's someone I'd like you to meet," he said. "This is Zo, one of the Red Balconies' companions. Zo, this is Governor Loukianos."

"Prince Zoharaza?" said Loukianos.

CHAPTER 15

ZO HAD NEVER MET the man in front of him, that he could recall, but that wasn't too surprising. Plenty of people had once known him by sight whom he had never noticed or known by name himself. To tell the truth, he'd lived the last five years always expecting this moment to come and being pleasantly surprised when it didn't.

"I go by Zo these days," he said, smiling. He'd always wondered what he would say, and that was what it turned out to be.

"But you are Zoharaza," the governor pursued, "aren't you? The son of King Chahaz of Satasparsa? You were at the court of the King of Zash in Rataxa, ten years ago, as a hostage. I used to see you at the royal audiences."

"Ah, did you? What a coincidence."

He couldn't look at Hylas. How could he, after concealing something like this from him? What excuse could he give? He couldn't expect Hylas to accept the truth.

"So you are Prince Zoharaza." The governor was not going to let this go, damn his eyes.

"Yes."

"Blessed Orante! I thought I might be going mad for an instant there." He laughed heartily.

"Not at all, sir," said Zo smoothly. He gestured to the divan beside him. "Will you join me?"

The governor sat, and Hylas, whose eyes Zo still could not meet, sat beside him.

"Ought you to call me 'sir'?" Loukianos wondered. "You wouldn't have, ten years ago—and I would have called you … what would I have called you? You're a prince, but not one of the royal sons of Zash … Did you have a title at the court?"

"'Your Grace,' as a courtesy in formal settings. But you were a foreigner, and probably of high rank yourself?"

"Mm, not at the time, no, I was just the son of an engineer in the colonial legions. Got to stay at the court for a while because of some family connections. What a place it was!"

"Indeed, sir."

"But how did you end up here?"

"I was shipwrecked near Tykanos five years ago."

"Blessed Orante! The stuff of romantic fiction. So you left the court five years ago," said Loukianos thoughtfully. "Let me see, who can I ask about?"

There was much conversation to be had along those lines, while the governor reminisced about his time in Zash, asking Zo if he remembered such-and-such, whether he'd ever known so-and-so and what had become of him, recalling lurid court plots that he had known of, food that he had eaten, and gardens that he had visited. It was certainly true, as Hylas had said, that they had a lot to talk about.

Hylas himself remained silent, but he did not leave. He lit a stick of incense for himself and one for the governor, and he returned to sit with Loukianos and Zo, cradling his wine cup and listening to them talk. In the crowded sitting room, it was not rude; the governor and Zo were not having a private conversation. And Loukianos would include him every so often, turning to Hylas to say, "Isn't that remarkable?" or "That's what it's really like, you know."

So it was official. Prince Zoharaza, dead five years ago by his own hand, was back in the world.

"What a delight to get to talk about Rataxa with someone who was there," Loukianos said as he was taking his leave. "I'm so glad Hylas convinced me to come tonight. Shall we?" He turned to Hylas, and then recollected himself. "Ah, I forgot, you live here! You won't be coming with me. Well, I'll bid you both good night, then." And he bowed, Zashian-style, the appropriate degree for someone of Zo's rank.

Zo got up from the divan, staggering in his haste. He knew that the moment Loukianos was gone, the few remaining regular guests and the other companions would descend on him, full of questions and amazement. He wouldn't even blame them. But he didn't want to face it.

Hylas would not ask questions. He would probably melt away while the others crowded around.

"Are you all right?" Loukianos asked, looking back at Zo.

"I'm fine—sitting too long, that is all."

"You're too young to have stiff knees," said the governor jovially.

"Nevertheless. And I'm off to bed."

Loukianos laughed. "Too young for that, too."

They walked out onto the gallery together, and Loukianos did not offer Zo his arm because Zo did his best not to look like he needed it. On the gallery they parted ways, and Zo waited until the governor was halfway down the outer stairs and not looking in his direction before he took hold of the railing to steady himself as he walked around to the back stairs.

The back stairs were in total darkness. There was a window in the stairwell which would have let in some moonlight, but it had shutters which someone had closed, and Zo couldn't even make out the outline of where it was. There was no way he could descend the stairs without a light.

He wanted to be in his bed, in his room with his door locked. He didn't want to walk all the way back along the gallery and meet someone else coming out of the sitting room to say, "Zo, are you really Prince Whatever like that man said?"

He sat down on the top step of the back stairs and put his head in his hands. Presently, a flicker out of the corner of his eye told him that someone was coming down the gallery with a light. Zo looked up wearily. It was Hylas.

He came to the head of the stairs and stopped.

"May I join you?" he said.

"What, here?"

"It's where you are."

"Of course." Zo shrugged.

Hylas set down the candle he was carrying and sat, not on the top step beside Zo but lower down. At Zo's feet.

He looked up at Zo, and the candlelight shone on his faded red hair and sparkled in his pale eyes. His smile was as warm as the flame's light.

"Of course you're a prince," he said, his voice low. "I feel as if I should have known."

"I should have told you."

"You could of course have told me at any time. I would have done with the knowledge only what you wanted. I hope you're not sorry for me to know now."

"No. No. But you shouldn't have found out that way. I didn't tell you because it doesn't matter. It's not an important thing."

Hylas nodded. "Of course it doesn't matter. I understand that. Except … " He looked up at Zo, and there was some-

155

thing in his eyes, a tense kind of joy. "Could we let it matter, a little?"

"How? What do you mean?" There was something new here, something thrilling. He couldn't say what it was.

"I could almost believe that this is what I was made a commoner for. I should not say that—the suffering my family went through because of me, I can never forget that. But it is in the past, and I have paid for it. Zo, will you let me serve you?"

"Will I … Hylas, you do, actually. All these things you've done for me … "

"I know. Will you let me keep serving you? And maybe … " He put out a hand toward Zo's hand and very gently, tentatively, laced their fingers together. "In new ways?"

Zo gasped and squeezed Hylas's hand tight. "Holy God, *yes*. Hylas, I thought you would never ask."

Hylas hadn't thought beyond that moment. He certainly wasn't prepared to act, now, on what he'd just proposed, but he realized that it was expected of him. Well, of course it was.

As he'd sat and listened to Zo and Loukianos talk, the absurd thought that kept rattling around in his head was: *He's a prince. I should give him what he wants.*

It was absurd because whatever Zo was a prince of, it had never mattered to Hylas, even in his former life. It certainly didn't matter here, far from Zo's homeland, and it changed nothing between them. And it was absurd because he knew —he thought he knew—what Zo wanted. He wanted their friendship to expand beyond tea and buns and their shared garden; he wanted something from Hylas that Hylas could easily, joyfully give. Of course he should have it.

"Then would you like me to give you a kiss?" he whispered.

"I would, very much."

Hylas nodded. He reached up to touch Zo's face with the tips of his fingers, as if he needed to do this to guide himself to Zo's lips. He was shocked by how intimate it felt. He moved the edge of his thumb over Zo's cheek.

"I may not be very good at this," he warned, and before Zo could say something comforting in reply, he knelt up to bring his lips to Zo's and brushed them across, a little parted.

His body felt alight with the thrill of that contact. He did it again, softening his mouth against Zo's. Zo received his kisses like a pool filling with water, effortlessly welcoming.

Eventually Hylas drew back, knowing that by some miracle, even though he had dared so little, he had done well. He could see that in the way Zo was looking at him.

Still he was not quite prepared for Zo to slide down off the top step into his lap. Hylas stiffened with surprise, Zo's whole soft, warm body suddenly in his arms. Reflexively, Hylas hugged him to his chest. Zo gripped his shoulders and shook with laughter, surprised in his turn.

"I was just going to kiss you again," Zo said.

"Sorry." Hylas let go of him.

"No." Zo snuggled against him. "This is good too. This is … I've wanted this from you too."

Hylas tightened his embrace again, and Zo tucked his head down against Hylas's shoulder. They stayed like that until Zo moved against Hylas, reaching up to kiss him. This kiss was luscious and melting, Zo's tongue slipping into Hylas's mouth.

Zo drew back just enough to look into Hylas's eyes. His beautiful eyebrows rose in a question.

"Yes," Hylas replied. And it was touching to be checked on like this, a man of his age, but he couldn't help making light of it too. "I can take it, Your Grace."

Zo wrinkled his nose, and then he was kissing Hylas again, deep, mastering kisses. They panted against each other's mouths. Hylas, unthinking, found himself cupping his hands under Zo's rear to lift him up for a better angle. He almost let go in shock when he realized what he'd done, but the way Zo reacted, twining his arms around Hylas's neck and kissing him forcefully, made it impossible to feel he had made a mistake.

Snatches of moralizing he had heard in his youth jostled in his mind: *Men who would let themselves be penetrated like a fortress falling to the enemy ... Always be like the sword, not like the scabbard ...* It was just kissing, but it felt like that, exactly like that, and he loved it.

A door opened somewhere, and there were voices down the gallery. Zo jerked back, and Hylas quickly caught him by the waist and set him back down on the step. Zo snatched up the candle Hylas had brought and shielded its light with his hand.

"Let's go downstairs," Zo whispered.

Hylas held out one hand to help Zo up and took the candle with the other so that Zo could gather up his robe to stand, and they made their way quietly down the stairs.

In the little anteroom outside their two doors, they paused.

"It's been a long day for you," said Hylas, "and I think you're tired. I wouldn't want to ... add to that. Shall I see you in the morning?"

Zo sighed. "I am tired," he admitted. "I want you, but I'm tired. Sometimes I hate my body."

"Well ... I don't. I don't know if that helps. May I come in and put you to bed, Your Grace?"

That made Zo laugh, as Hylas had hoped it would. He followed Zo into his room, lit the lamp for him, pulled back the curtain and took down his sleeping robe, then kissed him good night and left him sitting on the edge of his bed to go out through the garden door.

158

He was back in the morning, at the usual time. Their time, he thought—perhaps that made it fitting. He'd smiled and nodded when the kitchen staff asked him excitedly if he'd heard that their very own Zo was a prince.

He had hardly slept, his mind too busy processing the events of that evening, going over everything that had happened, everything that it meant. He felt fresh and alert, as if he'd slept long and deeply.

There was a bird singing in the garden, and the sun felt warm on Hylas's face, in spite of the chill in the air—the world replying in small, tentative ways to the joy and anticipation in his heart. He looked toward Zo's door just as it slid open.

"Good morning," said Zo.

"Good morning," said Hylas, "my prince."

Zo beamed. His hair was loose over his shoulder, tousled with sleep, his robe carelessly tied at the waist, his feet bare. He looked like a prince—he always had, in fact, and Hylas wondered why it had come as a surprise to anyone that that was what he was.

"Come in?" Zo gestured behind him.

Hylas nodded. He was suddenly seized with nerves; his hands on the tea tray shook, and the bowls rattled betrayingly. Zo's gaze on him was gentle.

They entered Zo's room, leaving the garden door open behind them. Sunlight spilled over Zo's rumpled bed. Hylas set the tray down on the table, but he did not sit, unsure what to do next, what was appropriate. Perhaps he should not have brought the tea and buns at all.

Zo was stooping over the table, catching up the trailing sleeve of his robe, in that enchanting way he had, in order to pick up the pot and pour tea into the two bowls, filling each less than halfway. He passed one to Hylas, straightening up and reaching across the table.

"Shall we sit and drink?" he said, lifting his own bowl and looking at Hylas through the steam.

Hylas sipped his tea, still standing. "I, uh … Do you want to?"

Zo sipped his tea. "Not really."

"Neither do I," said Hylas quickly. "I just brought the tea because … "

"Because you always bring me tea," Zo finished for him.

Hylas nodded. "And I am certainly not going to stop now."

Zo took another sip of his tea and set the bowl down on the table. He tugged at the tie holding his robe closed, and it slipped easily open. He wore nothing under it. The soft fabric of the robe slid back over his shoulders to his elbows. He stepped into the sunlight from the open door and smiled at Hylas.

Old instinct made Hylas tense and want to look away. He tightened his hands around the warm bowl of tea.

"I—I don't want you to get cold," he said absurdly.

"It's warm in the sun," said Zo, "and I am from the mountains of Eastern Zash. I can withstand the cold better than you might think."

The sunlight glowed all down the side of his bare skin, the swoop and angle of his neck and shoulder, his smooth bare chest, the supple juncture of hip and groin and round thigh. His manhood was full, pink-tinted, and thick with desire. Hylas's knees felt weak.

He set down the bowl of tea.

"What should I do?" he said, stepping into the sunlight. "You—you'll have to tell me, I'm afraid."

"I've been looking forward to it."

Zo held out a hand, and when Hylas took it, he drew him closer, tipping back his head to invite a kiss. Hylas kissed

160

him carefully, forced by his height to be the tentative initiator.

"I love the way you do that," Zo murmured against Hylas's lips. He still held one of Hylas's hands, and now he lifted it and pressed it to his chest. "Touch me."

"I—I am, it seems."

He kissed Zo again, cupping Zo's face with his other hand, Zo's skin cool under his fingers. He ran his hand down Zo's chest to his soft belly, palmed the gentle angle of his hip, slipped in under the fabric of Zo's robe to cup the perfect curve of his rear. Zo's arms twined around his neck. They swayed together as they kissed again, each pulling the other in, and Zo made an undulating motion of his hips that rubbed the heat of his arousal against Hylas's, with only the fabric of Hylas's clothing between them.

Hylas gasped, clutching at Zo's delicate flesh. He felt himself almost on the verge of climax just from that little wriggle. That would not do. Zo would want more—deserved much more.

He was clasping a young man's naked body to himself, his desire blatant, and he was not ashamed. But this was Zo, his dear friend, his beloved, for whom he would do anything.

"Can I—can I carry you to the bed?" Hylas whispered, his throat dry.

"Mm. Please do."

He scooped Zo up, the way he had done the night before on the stairs, hands under his ass. Zo wrapped his legs around Hylas's waist, and it was easy to carry him the few steps to his bed. There Hylas had some idea of setting him down and then sinking to his knees on the floor in front of him, awaiting instructions. But Zo didn't let go of him, and they tumbled down onto the bed together.

"Ah! My prince, I—"

"Something wrong?" Zo froze, suddenly attentive.

He was lying between Zo's naked thighs, chest-to-chest,

Zo's arms around his shoulders, in the warm sunlight on Zo's rumpled bed.

"No," he admitted.

They kissed wildly, Zo's mouth wet and eager, Hylas's hands travelling over his body in long strokes. Now Zo was undoing Hylas's belt and pulling his tunic off over his head, somehow without quite breaking their embrace. He ran his fingertips through the hair on Hylas's chest as they kissed, smoothed his palm down Hylas's bare back.

Hylas rolled onto his side to catch his breath and steady himself. He could do this, he told himself; it was a thing that required no great skill, and Zo would be gracious about it, no matter what happened. The thought comforted him.

He snuggled close to Zo and reached his hand down between their bodies to touch Zo's manhood. It was hot and heavy and silk-smooth, and Zo gave a low moan when Hylas touched it. There—Hylas had known he would be gracious. He handled Zo's member gently, a much slower version of the motions he used on himself when he needed release. His wrist rubbed against his own arousal, trapped inside his undergarment.

He looked into Zo's face, seeking encouragement. Zo's eyes were heavy-lidded, his head thrown back on the pillow, lips a little parted. For a wild moment Hylas felt as if he should look away, as if he should not see his prince like this, so abandoned to pleasure.

He stroked slower, and Zo spread his thighs and moved his hips, pushing into Hylas's hand. He began to wriggle more urgently, and Hylas knew it meant he needed to speed up. He managed to hook his loincloth with his thumb and jerk the fabric out of the way—his other arm was trapped under Zo—and they were touching, heat to heat, and he caressed them both together. He could do this easily; he had big hands.

He had strong thighs, too, to hold him up as his moved

over Zo, rocking against him, rubbing their bodies together while his hand moved between them, slick with their first emissions. Zo's hands slid down Hylas's back and over his rear, fingers spread. It was bliss; it was more than he deserved. But if Zo felt anything like this building ecstasy—he couldn't stop, it *was* right, it was perfect, because Zo deserved everything. Hylas bit his lip to try to silence his own noises, but they came out of him like sobs, and that felt good too.

Then Zo's body stiffened, and before Hylas could gasp out a panicked "What's wrong?" he heard Zo's cry of satisfaction and felt Zo's seed spill over his hand, and realized what had happened. On a wave of overwhelming relief and gratitude he reached his own climax and clasped Zo to himself so that they both came together, legs tangled, arms wrapped around each other, faces buried in one another's necks.

CHAPTER 16

THEY LAY IN THE SUNLIGHT, which slanted in the open door at just the right angle to warm the bed. Zo gathered his robe loosely around himself and looked at Hylas lying naked beside him. Hylas's pale eyes were on him, questioning.

"Was it ... satisfying?" Hylas asked anxiously. "Your Grace?"

Zo laughed. "Very satisfying. You must have been able to tell."

"Well ... yes."

He'd only exaggerated his pleasure a very little, out of a combination of habit and affection. It really had been lovely.

"You know what you're doing. I thought you said you didn't."

"Ah, well, I ... "

Zo patted Hylas's bare stomach casually and felt Hylas stiffen with surprise. "I know how you learned to do that," he said, not wanting to make Hylas explain that the only cock he'd ever handled was his own. There was probably some taboo in the stupid place he was from. "I'm teasing you."

Hylas relaxed, turning to nestle closer against Zo's side.

"Zoharaza," he said slowly.

"Yes?"

"Oh. I was just trying to say it. Did I get it right, then?"

"Almost. The second 'z' should have more of a 'zzz' to it."

"Ah. I'll remember."

"You don't have to. 'Zo' is fine."

"Mm. I do think I should be able to pronounce your full name properly. It's basic, you know?"

"Prince Zoharaza, Son of Chahaz Son of Temar, Kings of Satasparsa and the Eastern Peaks. That's the Zashian style, but we're from the Parkan really, and there was a different style at home, which ... I don't remember, actually. It's been so long since I was there."

"Loukianos said you were a hostage at the King of Sasia's court. But that didn't mean a prisoner in a cell, did it?"

"No ... I lived as a member of the king's household, with his wives and children. But I was ten years old when I arrived. I was never going to forget that I didn't really belong there—and no one else was going to forget, either. And of course none of us had freedom to come and go completely at will—or to leave the palace, obviously."

"So a little bit like here."

Zo laughed. "A *little* bit. The palace I lived in was bigger than the town of Tykanos—including the fort—with more people in it. And it's not even the biggest of the king of Zash's palaces. And we could go into the gardens, which were probably the size of this island, and the hunting park ... not alone, you couldn't really do anything alone, no one could, but ... it wasn't like being a prisoner in a cell."

"But you still ran away."

Zo looked at him. "I never said that."

"No, you never said it. I'm sure everyone else thinks you were supposed to be on the ship that was wrecked off the coast of Tykanos. You were the only survivor, or something—perhaps you had amnesia for a while ... "

"Amnesia! Why didn't I think of that?"

"I don't know. You should have talked to me first. No—I don't mean that. You kept your own counsel, and I don't begrudge you that in the least. I daresay … you were used to needing to."

"Holy God, you've no idea. You couldn't trust *anyone*. Even the people … even the people who were trustworthy could be turned against you by your enemies. And I had enemies. I was a boy, not a courtier, and I tried not to offend anyone—I made a study of it, how to be charming to everyone—but I still had enemies, because of who I was, who my father was.

"I wouldn't have run away. The thought never entered my head. I was well provided for. I missed my family, but I had —thought I had—friends at the king's court. I'd started to have love affairs. I'm courtier material—I thought I was. And I was being useful to my father, in the best way I could be, as a hostage for his good behaviour. You might think it sounds unfeeling of him to give me up, as if he must not have cared for me, but it wasn't like that. I was a favourite, his youngest —he'd have loved to keep me with him, but he had to send me. My eldest brothers were men already, and he needed them at home. My middle brother was a troublemaker, and I'm sure my father would have liked to send him away, but you can't give your problem child as a hostage to your sovereign, how would that look? I was the obvious choice, so I offered to go."

"You were a good son." Hylas squeezed his shoulder, a chaste gesture although they were lying there half-clothed and sticky with semen. Zo wondered if he was being an idiot, spoiling the mood like this. It was the poor man's very first time having sex.

"I tried to be." There was no help for it now, and he doubted Hylas minded, really. He was so serious himself. "Anyway, I told you I fell ill when I was fifteen and never got better—I didn't tell you what made me sick in the first place."

"No ... " said Hylas on an indrawn breath.

"Yeah. I was poisoned. It was like that there—that was the kind of thing that happened. I think it was meant to kill me, but they miscalculated, maybe, got the dose wrong because I was small and slight and they thought I would succumb easily." He shrugged, and Hylas's hand tightened on his shoulder again. "I survived and got better, sort of, but my health was never the same, and I knew that left me vulnerable to other attacks. I was pretty sure I knew who did it, and why—it was a problem that I knew wasn't going to go away. As I saw it, I had three choices. I could do nothing and probably be killed, and my family wouldn't benefit from that. I could fight back, become a poisoner and an intriguer myself—and if I got caught, it would be ruin for my family, and if I didn't, I'd probably end by having to betray a friend or a lover. I'd already seen that happen to other people. Or I could run away.

"It took me nearly a year to find a way to get a message safely to my father to ask his permission, or warn him that I was going to do it—I'm not quite sure which I was doing. But he sent back immediately an embroidered coat, a specific kind of coat that you give your sons in the Parkan as a token of your blessing, when they leave home. He'd given me one when I left the first time, but he sent me another one. I knew that meant that whatever I did, he'd handle the result, that he wanted me to go and live. But I think it also meant I couldn't go home—which I knew, of course.

"The actual leaving of the king's palace wasn't hard. I just had to bribe some people and know the right place to sneak out—a complex that big can't be guarded as well as all that. I staged a bit of a fake suicide, as if I'd drowned myself in the artificial lake—I left some clothes on the shore and wrote a note. I don't know that it would have held up for long, but it didn't need to, and in that place, it was much more likely they'd suspect someone had killed or kidnapped me than that I had run away.

"I made my way to the coast and got on a ship headed for Glif, not for any particular reason—by then I was exhausted and sick, and I got on the first ship I could that was going far enough away. I could have continued on to Glif after that ship was wrecked here, if I'd wanted to, but I just didn't bother. It wasn't a dramatic wreck. We ran aground on some rocks, but the ship didn't sink, and everyone was ferried to shore with all our luggage. A couple of my fellow passengers brought me here—I'd been unwell the whole voyage and couldn't really fend for myself—and Theano had me put in this room, which they were renting out just like your room at the time. I stayed until my health improved, but by then I'd begun to feel at home here. I was already more or less working for the house. I'd go out in the evenings and sit in the courtyard and chat with the guests, sometimes play my flute. I flirted with people, I drank tea. It was like the good parts of life at the Zashian court without anyone trying to poison or backstab or intrigue with you. Very much. I mean, they do intrigue here, or they think they do, but angels of the Almighty, it's amateur stuff, Hylas. It's quaint."

Hylas chuckled. "I don't think we Pseuchaians are very good at intrigue."

"You're really not. I like that about you."

"So you found a home here, and you decided to stay."

"I guess I did. I guess … the only thing that was missing was … "

He felt tears suddenly, out of nowhere, stinging in his eyes. What was that about? He reached for Hylas's arm, pulled it by the wrist to draw it over his body. Hylas obediently gathered him in.

"What was missing?" Hylas asked innocently.

"Someone I could open my heart to. Trusting … " He

was crying in earnest now. "Trusting them not to betray me. I never—I never had that. I never told anyone all this. And I just did, just now. It's you, Hylas. You are the only thing that was missing. Please don't betray me."

He shouldn't have said it. It showed weakness and wouldn't make a difference. But it also didn't need saying. This was the man who hadn't allowed himself to leave Ariata and live fully as himself until all his duties to his family were discharged and half his own life was over. He didn't need to be taught anything about loyalty. He deserved someone who could trust him unquestioningly.

He hugged Zo to his chest and kissed the top of Zo's head.

"Never, Zo. Never. I can't promise not to disappoint you or that I can give you everything you deserve. But betray you? No. You can trust me. I'll tell you so as often as you need to hear it."

Zo snuffled against Hylas's chest and let himself be held tightly for a little while before he wiped his face and rolled over to sit up. Hylas released him, pushing himself up on one elbow. Zo drew a deep breath and let it out slowly.

"I was going to apologize, but I guess it's rather special, being the first person to be trusted with someone's secrets."

"Incredibly special. Frightening, even. Though—I promise I can handle it."

Zo smiled down at him. "Let us get up and eat our breakfast. There is still a world out there, and I suppose we should face it."

In fact, there was plenty for Hylas to do in the world outside the Red Balconies. He had plans to tackle another of the broken water pipes on the edge of town, which meant scrounging up a work crew from somewhere. Then he had an appointment with Mutari in the afternoon, mostly to return the copy of *The Bronze Dolphin* that he had borrowed from her.

He had never imagined how it would feel to do any of that after having made love to Zo first thing in the morning.

He felt changed by the experience, but somehow less so than he would have imagined. No one asked him, "What are you smiling about?" or "What's gotten into you?" and that didn't seem strange; he didn't think he showed any outward signs of the transformation inside him.

But he thought about Zo so much that day that it was distracting. When he was waiting to speak to a clerk at the government office, he was remembering the feeling of running his hand over Zo's thigh. When he was supposed to be assessing the state of the pipe that had been dug up under the road, he was thinking about the way Zo's tongue had felt in his mouth.

He almost couldn't bring himself to remember how it had felt to touch Zo's prick. He had done it, he had touched it extensively, explored its shape, rubbed it against his own ... It still felt wrong to dwell on it—as if he might have made it less real by not thinking about it.

He stopped dead in the street outside the House of the Peacock when he had that thought. He wanted it to have been entirely real. He would make a point of thinking about it deliberately, just to spite whatever impulse from his upbringing was telling him he shouldn't—just maybe not right now, because right now he was outside the House of the Peacock and due to be drinking tea with Mutari.

Mutari had news, and surprisingly, it had to do with the aqueduct, which Hylas had almost forgotten about.

"Supposedly the new envoy from Glif is on the island already," she told him, "incognito."

"Really?"

She shrugged. "It doesn't *sound* credible, but I heard it

from a reliable source in Tetum. I don't know what he's doing. Perhaps he doesn't trust Loukianos, or perhaps he just wanted to enjoy the tea houses at his leisure before taking up his post."

"Do you think Loukianos knows?"

"Well. That's a question. Are you going to tell him, if he doesn't?"

"No. He doesn't need to get his gossip from me."

Mutari laughed. "That's true. He has many other sources. I daresay he knows all about it already—it may be that the envoy went straight to him and is only 'incognito' to the rest of us."

"Well, then, he doesn't know how business should be done on Tykanos," said Hylas loyally. "You've got to introduce yourself at the tea houses *first*. Don't you?"

"Absolutely. Hylas, you're so much more at home here than you were when I first met you."

"I can't imagine leaving," Hylas said, and it was true.

Yet if they couldn't build the aqueduct, how long could he afford to stay? There was work to do, work that made use of his skills, but nobody was paying him to do it.

And Zo needed a patron. That fact had taken on an entirely different colour since last night.

He realized he'd missed something Mutari had said as he grappled with his thoughts.

"Yes, I think so," he answered more or less at random. "Mutari, this garland that the companions talk about … "

She accepted the change of topic easily. "For patronage, you mean?"

"Yes, that. What is it, exactly?"

"A crown of greenery. Flowers sometimes—there's symbolism to the different plants, but of course it also depends on the time of year you want to offer it. Are you thinking of making it official with someone?"

He looked at her. By now he thought he knew her well

enough that he could tell she didn't really believe he was. She would have been more excited about it if she had.

He smiled. "No, of course not. I was just wondering."

"So did you have amnesia?" was the first thing Chrestos asked when he met Zo coming out of the men's bath that morning. "And did it all come flooding back when the governor recognized you? What does that feel like?"

"I have no idea. I didn't have amnesia."

"Oh." Chrestos looked disappointed. "So you mean you've known you were a prince this whole time?"

"All my life."

"Why didn't you tell us? Did you think we wouldn't believe you? I would have. Are you going to go back and inherit the throne or whatever now?"

"No. I'm not that kind of prince. And I'm in exile."

It was a line he had decided on before leaving his room, knowing he'd need it. The best part about it was that it was sort of true. He didn't need to explain that he had exiled himself.

He was looking forward to telling Hylas the clever solution he'd come up with when he saw him again. Would he come and burn incense that evening? Zo would like to think that he would, that he wouldn't be able to wait until tomorrow morning.

"Well, I don't know exactly what that means," Chrestos was saying, spoiling the effect somewhat, "but Mistress is going to want to know why you haven't been telling all the guests about being a prince. She's going to think she can start a bidding war between Timon of Kos and Governor Loukianos over who gets to offer you a garland." He frowned thoughtfully. "Actually I guess I *can* see why you haven't been telling people."

That was how Zo spent the rest of his morning, telling bits of the truth about his past. The women companions, who were better read in Zashian literature than Chrestos, had little difficulty filling in the gaps that he left vague.

"Of course you don't want to go back!" Taris said. "No one's really free in a royal court, are they?"

"Like birds in a gilded cage," said Menthe wisely. "That's what I've heard."

The best winter sitting room was packed with guests that night. Mistress Aula was still away, staying with her friend who had just given birth. The lamplight flickered over Pani and Menthe's murals, and Zo was playing his flute when Hylas came in, arm in arm with the new Zashian regular, Nahaz. They caused a minor commotion by the door, and Zo almost faltered in the notes of his song. Nahaz was hatless and dishevelled, holding his head as if in pain, and Hylas supported him to a divan, where he collapsed gratefully, and Taris flew to his side. Zo went on playing, more quietly—no one was listening to him now, but they would notice if he stopped—and watched Hylas depart dutifully on some errand at Taris's command. He was curious, of course, but he knew he'd hear all about it in due course. For the moment he was content to enjoy watching Hylas be helpful to other people.

Eventually Hylas came and sat with the group near Zo, and Zo heard the story of what had happened to Nahaz. Hylas had met him outside of one of the other tea houses, where Nahaz had been trying to break up a fight between two other guests and got himself knocked down in the street. Hylas had come to his aid and, he admitted after some prompting, succeeded in both breaking up the fight and rescuing Nahaz.

"I thought to bring him here, because, erm … "

"Naturally you would bring him here," said one of Zo's regulars. "Where better?"

"Well, I live here, you see," Hylas elaborated. "I'm the tenant. I just thought to bring him back to the kitchen to get cleaned up. It was his idea to come up here—he said he wanted to see Taris."

Zo smiled, wondering if that was quite true. It was natural for Hylas to bring the injured man home with him, and no doubt if Nahaz had wanted to go straight to the kitchen, Hylas would have taken him there. But Zo could easily imagine that the idea of going up to see Taris had been offered as an alternative by Hylas himself. He was learning that kind of subtlety. Zo was so proud of him.

For a moment in the crowded, lamplit sitting room, Zo was captured by a vivid memory from that morning: Hylas naked in his bed, so intent as he moved over Zo, the look in his eyes saying that he cared as much for Zo's pleasure as for his own, if not more. Zo shivered, and two of his regulars asked simultaneously if he was cold.

Hylas lingered after the guests cleared out, helping Pani and Chrestos stack cushions and extinguish lamps. It seemed very natural. Taris had disappeared with Nahaz, whether still reminding him of his mother or not, Zo didn't know or care to know.

"Who's Mistress going to have entertaining in the public sitting rooms," Chrestos mused aloud, "if all the rest of you get patrons? I mean, they'll want you to themselves all the time."

"Not necessarily," said Zo. "That's how you and Captain Themistokles are, but … "

"It's not that he's jealous! He's not, you know. He doesn't mind my entertaining other men when he's not here. So long as it's not in private, of course."

"I know," said Zo soothingly. It was just that Themistokles wasn't very sociable. He didn't want to offend Chrestos by pointing that out. "That's his preference. Some men like to meet in company as well as in private. But—you do have a point. Mistress is so desperate for us to pair off, but she's not thinking about what it will do to the entertainment." He shrugged. "I guess she'll find out."

"But what if she takes us down that path, and it ruins the house?" Chrestos pursued. "We can't let her do that. It's our house, too."

"We won't let it happen," said Hylas simply.

"That's right," said Pani, around a yawn. "Listen to the aqueduct man, Chrestos. Let's all get to bed."

Hylas walked down the gallery with Zo. It still seemed natural. They were going to the same part of the house, after all. Hylas had the lamp. At the top of the stairs, he offered his hand to Zo, as he might have done any time in the last four months, and Zo took it, as he might have done, and their bodies settled together in a way that they would not have done any time before that morning.

They'd taken two steps down the stairs when Chrestos appeared on the top step behind them.

"Do you—" he started, and froze.

"What?" Zo asked, looking up.

They were just holding hands; Hylas was helping him down the stairs. Of course they were going to brazen it out.

"Nothing. I can keep a secret," Chrestos blurted, and wheeled away like a soldier on parade.

"Can he, do you think?" Hylas asked after they had stood there on the stairs for a long moment, listening to Chrestos's retreating footsteps.

"I doubt it. But we can always claim he misinterpreted what he saw." He looked up into Hylas's eyes, pale in the lamplight. "Though it would be nice not to have to."

"Would it?" Hylas looked half embarrassed, half amused.

"To say, 'The aqueduct man is my lover'? Yes, I would like that."

Hylas was silent a moment. "Zo from the Red Balconies is my lover," he said softly. "No one would believe it—but I would like to say it."

Chrestos had believed it—Chrestos had *guessed* it, Zo wanted to point out, and frankly, Chrestos wasn't usually the first to guess things. But he didn't say that. He didn't say how much it meant to him that Hylas had said "Zo from the Red Balconies" and not "Prince Zoharaza," either. He couldn't speak, because his throat seemed suddenly to be closing up at the thought that they *couldn't* say any of this. Whether Chrestos could keep their secret or not, it *was* a secret, it had to be, and to realize that both of them were wishing it need not be felt, for a moment, like the worst thing in the world.

It was Hylas who broke the silence to say gently, "We should go down to bed. To *our beds*, I mean. And then—I'll see you tomorrow morning?"

CHAPTER 17

THE WEATHER TURNED warm with the sunrise the next morning, and Zo was out in the garden, sitting in his chair, before Hylas arrived. Hylas had put him to bed the night before, kissing him good night with that tenderness that made Zo's knees feel weak in a surprisingly good way.

Hylas came out with his tray of tea and buns as usual, but he stopped outside his door and stood looking at Zo with his wistful smile for a long moment.

"I wondered if you'd be out here," he said, "since it's so pleasant."

Zo stretched luxuriantly in his chair. "The winters are so short here. I just start to brace myself for the real cold, and then it never comes, and the whole thing is over."

Hylas came and took his usual spot by Zo's chair, setting the tea tray on the ground. After a moment's hesitation, he laid his hand on Zo's knee, a tentative, light touch. He looked up into Zo's face.

"It is good to see you in your garden again," he said. "You make it more beautiful."

Zo shifted the fabric of his robe, which was loosely belted

and opened at the front. He tugged it out from under Hylas's hand so that his palm lay on bare skin. He waited for the reaction, wondering if it would be shock—"Not out here!"—or solicitude—"You're not wearing anything underneath? You will get cold!"

It was neither. Hylas looked up at him for a moment, frozen. Then he looked down, intent, as he ran his hand slowly up Zo's thigh. He bent his head to put his lips to Zo's skin, brushing them across in a kind of inchoate kiss. He touched the other side of Zo's robe, lifting the fabric slightly, and looked up at Zo for permission. In answer, Zo unfastened the tie that held his robe closed. He let Hylas fold back the other half of the robe himself.

Zo leaned back in his chair, bared to the gentle sunlight in his garden, and twined one leg around Hylas's shoulder to pull him closer.

"This is not uncomfortable for you, my love?" Hylas's voice was rough, his long, calloused hands warm on Zo's body but stilled as he waited for an answer.

"Not at all."

Hylas bent to stroking and kissing Zo's thighs and belly, his hands and mouth gentle and undemanding. Zo looked down the landscape of his own body, feeling like something precious under Hylas's reverent touch. Hylas was breathing hard, almost panting, as if he were the one being touched.

He probably thought of himself as fumbling, but to Zo just then he looked powerful, a man with the self-control to wait decades with this fire of yearning banked inside him and still, when he finally allowed himself this, to put his lover's needs before his own.

He nuzzled Zo's still-soft cock with his lips and then hesitantly slipped out his tongue to lick. Zo made an encouraging noise. He let Hylas explore raptly for a while, longer than he thought he could bear this kind of slow build-up, but that morning it was just what he needed. When he was fully hard, he reached down and wrapped Hylas's long fingers around the base of his cock.

"Just put the tip in your mouth and suck," he instructed.

Hylas looked up, cheeks flushed, lips red. "Just the tip?"

"Well. To start."

Hylas nodded obediently. Zo found himself lifted up, Hylas's hand under his ass—holy angels, he really liked that manoeuvre, didn't he—his legs draped over Hylas's shoulders, his whole cock in Hylas's mouth. He clutched the arms of the chair and moaned, levering his body up, pushing into the wet heat of Hylas's mouth.

"Ah! Keep going—you don't need any instructions, you beautiful man."

He really didn't. He'd only needed to be pointed in the right direction, and he sucked Zo with raw eagerness. In broad daylight, in Zo's garden. Zo looked up at the white clouds in the sky. The wind rustled the olive leaves. He writhed in Hylas's grasp, shouting aloud his need, totally abandoned to it, no longer even speaking Pseuchaian.

"God—angels—oh, Hylas, don't stop! No! Stop, slow down—"

And of course Hylas couldn't understand any of that, and Zo came, arching his back and clinging to the arms of the chair and swallowing a cry that would have echoed off the mountainside if he had let it out.

He also came in Hylas's mouth, and Hylas gulped it down. He released Zo's wet cock and set him gently back down in the chair. Then he sat back on the grass and fumbled for the tea things, pouring himself a bowl and taking several quick sips.

"It's not that ... I don't like the way you taste. I love it." He wiped his mouth, chest heaving, and swallowed another mouthful of tea. "It's just ... different."

"Mm," said Zo intelligently. He lay back in his chair, his robe still spread open, climax humming in his blood.

"Are you all right?"

"Mm. *Mmm.*"

Hylas chuckled. "Oh. I see." He sounded pleased with himself.

Hylas sat and ate buns and drank tea—or at least that was what Zo thought he was doing—while Zo stared at the sky a little longer.

"All right," said Zo finally, gathering himself up and pulling his robe around him. "It's your turn, my love." He reached out a hand invitingly.

Hylas started, swallowing a mouthful of pastry. "You don't have to call me that—and you don't have to—to—But you probably want to. You're very considerate. Don't get up, though. I'll—"

He sprang to his feet and pulled his tunic off over his head. He was bare underneath.

"You!" Zo was laughing. "You came out here with no—"

"So did you!" Hylas shot back, his cheeks flaming red.

"I'm a seductive and highly trained companion—you're a man who never had sex before yesterday!"

Hylas swallowed convulsively. "It won't always be like this," he said, and perhaps he was partly trying to reassure himself. He looked down at himself, naked and half aroused in the sunlight. "I'll be able to just sit with you the way we used to. But right now—I feel as if something has burst inside of me. I couldn't stop thinking about you all day yesterday. How it felt to touch you. I hope I am not making myself tedious."

"I never got to be part of anyone's initiation before." Zo got up from his chair and crossed the little space between them. He ran his hands down Hylas's spare, pale body as he spoke. "It's tremendous fun. But wouldn't you like to lie down on the grass?"

"I—I—would you like that? I would," he amended hastily, "if it's not uncomfortable for you."

Zo put his hands on Hylas's shoulders and gave him the slightest little push backward. Hylas's eyes went wide as he fell willingly back. He sank down awkwardly onto the grass, and Zo dropped down to join him.

"I've always wanted to do this," Zo admitted, touching Hylas's chest. "Outside, on the grass."

"You've only to say, my prince." Hylas covered Zo's hand with his own. "I am at your service."

His tone was light, his expression serious; he meant it, but not in the way another man might have meant it. Zo stored the moment away to muse on later.

He lay down, drawing Hylas to lie beside him. It was still slightly too cold for this, so they twined together, and Zo tugged his robe around them both. He explored Hylas's body lazily as he kissed him.

"Someday I will make you tell me what you've always wanted to do," Zo murmured. "And then I'll do it to you."

Hylas groaned, half-covering his face with one hand. Zo laughed and rolled them easily over in the grass so that he was on top of his lover, Hylas's lean thighs under his. He was getting hard again, as if making love to Hylas filled him up with vitality instead of draining him. He rubbed against Hylas, nuzzling with his lips at the fingers covering Hylas's face.

"Move your hand, I want to see your loveliness when you come."

Hylas made a noise between a sob and a laugh, but he did move his hand, reaching up to thread his fingers into Zo's hair. And he was lovely when he came, with Zo riding the swells of his pleasure. He squeezed his eyes shut and cried out, clutching at Zo's hip and bucking under him.

Zo moved his wet hand to his own cock, giving himself a few quick strokes to see if he had another climax in him. To his surprise, he did, a small but sweet one. He collapsed on top of Hylas, his head on Hylas's chest, delicious warmth spreading through his limbs. Birds sang up on the mountain, and the wind moved in the olive branches.

"I remember now," Zo mumbled after they had lain there for a while. "This is why I like sex. Because it can be like this."

"It's not always?" asked Hylas thickly.

"Mm. Not in my experience, no."

Hylas's hand was on Zo's back, stroking him through the fabric of his robe.

"You came twice," he remarked. "Does that happen often?"

"Almost never, for me. Making love in the morning after a good night's sleep seems a clever idea. Or maybe it's just making love to you."

Hylas kissed the top of Zo's head and shifted under him. "I can pour you some tea, if you move a little."

They moved, laughing, rolling onto one side so that Hylas could reach for the tea tray and fill Zo's bowl without breaking their sticky embrace. Zo propped himself on one elbow.

"Is it common to feel … a little silly afterwards?" Hylas asked.

Zo sipped his tea, which was still just warm. He'd never heard it put that way before, but now that he thought about it, feeling silly afterward would explain a lot of the bedroom behaviour he'd observed in some past lovers. The hasty retreats, the weird insults that came out of nowhere; it was how a certain type of man acted when he felt you'd made him look foolish.

"Mm. I think so, probably. But you don't have to. You're with a friend."

"I know." Hylas's smile was wide and sunny. He wasn't acting as if he felt anything but straightforwardly happy.

"I haven't had a friend become a lover before," Zo remarked lightly. "I didn't know what I was missing." He looked over his shoulder toward the tea tray, which was too far for him to reach. "Pass me the buns?"

Hylas untwined himself from Zo and sat up to grab the basket of buns and offer it. Zo selected one of Elpis's new flourless creations.

"What makes someone your lover?" Hylas asked.

Separated now, they didn't re-entwine themselves, though Zo wanted to. Hylas sat with his legs drawn up and his arms wrapped around his shins. Zo decided looking at him like this was a good consolation for not feeling his warmth. There were freckles on his elbows as well as his knees; Zo wasn't sure whether he'd noticed that before.

"I suppose … if both of us want to keep sleeping together, then we're lovers."

Hylas nodded. "That makes sense." He looked at the grass for a moment, thoughtful. "I had no idea that it would feel so … so *much*. So overwhelming. I thought … you'll laugh, but I really thought I was doing this mostly for you, because it was something you wanted."

Zo didn't laugh. "It was. It is. I'm glad you could tell. That's more than I could do—I didn't think you even thought of me that way."

"I didn't, at first. Ridiculous, isn't it? You're so lovely. It's not that I didn't notice. You must remember how I was when I first saw you—I could barely form words. But I'd buried my desires for so long, I didn't even recognize what I felt."

"My poor Hylas," Zo murmured, reaching out to stroke his cheek.

They took turns going to the men's bath, for the sake of discretion—no one saw either of them, so they needn't have bothered—and then sat on the divan in Zo's room until mid-morning, talking and laughing, touching and not touching, able to admit now how little they wanted to be apart. When Hylas finally got up to go, it was only because he felt guilty for taking up too much of Zo's time. He did not plan on even trying to do any work that day.

"Thanks for sitting with me for so long," Zo said, smiling up at him. "I'm a bit on edge, when I think about how many people might know who I am now."

"Oh, my prince!" Hylas dropped back down onto the divan and gathered Zo up in an awkward hug which Zo managed to smooth out, with a wriggle, into a comfortable embrace. "Do you want me to stay longer with you? I can stay if you want."

"No, I'm being irrational. You should go do things. I'll be here when you get back."

So he left, wandered around the market for a bit, bought some of the spiced nuts that Zo liked and a new writing tablet for himself, then went to the government office and spent a couple of hours staring out the window and rear-ranging things on his desk.

He felt like a man carrying around some secret knowl-edge, the location of buried treasure or the answer to an unsolved mystery of the universe. He'd lain with the most beautiful man on the island twice in two days. He knew what a man's seed tasted like—or at least what Zo's tasted like, because Zo had told him that different men tasted subtly different, and the thought that he, Hylas, had a lover who knew such things was unspeakably exhilarating. He knew what he wanted Zo to do to him, and soon he would work up the courage to ask, though he would make it clear that it could wait until Zo felt up to it, because he had an inkling that Zo's part might be strenuous. (He wanted to feel like a fortress taken by the enemy, like a scabbard with a sword very firmly rammed into it. He would come up with a less ridiculous way of expressing it.)

He was happy. He knew that his happiness couldn't last, but happiness never did, any more than pain. The only thing to do was the cherish it while you could.

CHAPTER 18

"If the governor goes, will you go with him?"

Hylas jolted out of his thoughts and stared at the man beside his desk. Dorios, the clerk. And Hylas could have sworn that was the first thing he had said; he was not so far gone in his reverie about Zo that he had missed a whole conversation.

"If the governor goes?" he repeated.

"Have you not heard the rumour, then? Oh, I thought you would have, being the governor's man. They're saying he's going to be recalled to Pheme."

"Who's saying that?" Hylas managed not to simply repeat "Recalled to Pheme?" like an idiot.

Dorios gestured around the office and listed some names. "Everyone I've talked to this morning. I don't know who started the rumour, but it's certainly spreading. So would you go with him, or … You'd be useful here, you know—I mean, quite apart from the aqueduct, which, it's a shame about that, but … "

He let the sentence hang unfinished. Hylas looked around the office and noticed that a number of people were surreptitiously paying attention to their conversation.

Dorios wasn't the only one who was interested in his answer. It was flattering, alarming, and not entirely unexpected.

"If Loukianos is recalled to Pheme," he said slowly, "I will stay and see if his successor has any better luck with the aqueduct."

"Good man!" said Dorios heartily.

Hylas left the office soon after that, as much to get away from everyone who was apparently interested in his future plans as anything. But he did also want to corner Loukianos and find out what was going on. His situation with the governor was such that he didn't really have much to fear from being blunt. The man had flirted with him, propositioned him, thrown up on him, and didn't pay him a salary. Perhaps it was only to be expected that he would be prepared to leave the island without telling Hylas.

Given the warm weather and the fact that he was possibly about to lose the governorship—and should probably have been doing something about that—Hylas expected to find Loukianos in his garden. He was right. He was shown to the couches in the grotto, and after a few minutes, Loukianos came strolling up in work clothes with dirt in his hair, pulling off leather gardening gloves.

"Hylas! What can I do for you?"

Hylas, who had been sitting on the edge of a couch without removing his sandals, stood up now.

"I heard a rumour this morning that the archons might recall you to Pheme."

"Ah." Loukianos nodded, not looking surprised. "Well. Yes. I heard the same rumour. I'm going to resign. I was going to send for you to tell you."

"Why?"

"Because I thought you should know."

"No, why are you going to resign?"

"Oh. Before I can be recalled, you know. It will look

better." He shrugged. "Maybe. A little. Here, let's sit. I'll—I'll tell you about it."

Loukianos toed off his sandals and flopped onto a couch, tossing his gloves at the table and missing. The slave who was present stooped to pick them up, and Loukianos sent him to bring them wine. Hylas resumed his seat on the edge of the couch opposite.

"I hadn't told you," Loukianos said, "but … the aqueduct project has been—it was communicated to me fairly clearly —my last chance to do something right on this island before the Phemian government decided I'd fucked up enough and appointed a new governor. There was an outbreak of dysentery at the fort last winter because of the water situation. They were drinking water meant for their bath house—I don't even know where that stuff comes from."

"The Eastern stream, heavily contaminated with runoff from the town fountains," said Hylas mechanically.

"Right. No wonder they got sick. No one died—it was all strong, young fellows who were affected, and they pulled through—luckily it didn't affect the town. But that was when I promised the aqueduct, and if I can't get it built, I'm finished. And it seems very much like I can't get it built."

"Why did you not tell me any of this sooner? Not about the dysentery—I found out about that my first week here. I assumed you didn't know."

"Of course I knew. It's my job. Which—I don't do very well, so fair point. No, I knew about that. Pheme knows about that—I figured you probably knew about it before you came here. I thought you probably knew my career was hanging by a thread. Because apparently when soldiers don't have enough sense not to drink their fucking bath water, it's the governor's fault. That was—partly—why I tried so hard to show you a good time when you first got here. I thought I needed to win you over."

Hylas stared at the mosaic beneath the table for a

moment. He was marshalling his thoughts, but before he could speak, one of Loukianos's slaves came in, followed by a couple of guests Hylas knew only vaguely, and the moment to speak had passed. Not that he thought anything he could have said would be likely to help, anyway.

He sat listening to Loukianos's guests chat about the tea houses and some gossip from Pheme, and the governor laughing and replying as if he hadn't just been telling Hylas that he was about to abandon the whole life he had built here without even a pretence of a fight.

Mistress Aula returned to the house that morning, and Zo made sure not to be there to hear the others tell her the news about him. The mistress had been subdued since Pani and Menthe revealed their frescoes, and Zo wasn't sure how he expected her to react. He also wasn't sure just how much about him she would hear. Would Chrestos mention what he had seen on the stairs? She came to his room after breakfast.

"Everyone is telling me that you're a prince. I'd think it was another of your pretences, but the *governor* recognized you from somewhere? And Chrestos tells me you haven't had amnesia or anything like that. So … "

Chrestos had not told her anything about him and Hylas, it would seem.

"So I have known all along who I am, and I concealed my identity on purpose. Yes."

"You must have a reason."

"I do. It's much as you might imagine."

She frowned at him.

He shrugged. "I have enemies. I am in exile, nobody knows where I am, and I'd like to keep it that way. But I wasn't—I'm not—a very important prince. Nobody is waiting for me to return in triumph and claim a throne. If that's what you were wondering."

"Of course it isn't. I'm *wondering* how I can turn this to the advantage of the house."

"You'd like to advertise the fact that one of your companions is foreign royalty."

"Of course. You must know you could have attracted more guests all these years if you hadn't kept it a secret."

He gritted his teeth. "But you also don't want me to leave."

She looked genuinely startled. "What? Who said anything about leaving? No one wants you to leave. You can't, anyway. Where would you go?"

She probably didn't even think she was saying anything sinister. These things just popped out of her mouth.

"I will have to find somewhere, won't I," he said coldly, "if you begin telling all the guests who I am."

Her eyes narrowed. "Are you threatening me?"

"You threatened me first."

"Well, so you'd leave. You're not really as ill as you pretend to be, then. I knew it."

All Zo's years of learning to resist this kind of nettling couldn't prevent anger surging in him.

"The only pretence I make about my health is that sometimes I pretend to be less sick than I feel. But I've long since stopped expecting you to have the decency to believe that."

Mistress Aula gave an exaggerated gasp. "You have the gall to talk about not being believed when you lied about *who you are* for five years?"

"I didn't, as a matter of fact. I haven't told any story about my past that isn't true. Zo isn't a made-up name—it's what my father called me when I was a boy, and I told Theano it was short for Zoharaza when I first got here. None of you thought I was an open book. It doesn't matter—believe what you like about me. I got here from Zash with this body, and I can get off the island with it if I have to. You can drive me to it or not, as you choose."

"Fine, if you think me a harpy, I will play the part." She surged to her feet, radiating indignation. "Get a garland from Governor Loukianos or Timon of Kos, I don't care which, by Orante's Month, or I'll spread your name—your title, your father's name, whatever it is you don't want people to know —about the whole island!"

Hylas could tell that Zo was tired that evening. He looked pale and seemed to have difficulty focussing on what his guests were saying; Hylas heard him ask people to repeat themselves, with very gracious apologies, a couple of times. He thought guiltily of their morning together and how much it might have cost Zo, when his strength was so limited. He wished he could move to sit beside Zo and offer his shoulder to rest against, help him keep up with the conversation, maybe even let him fall asleep for a little and take over his job of entertaining the guests. What an absurd thought.

All he could do was wait out the evening, lighting a second stick of incense that he could ill afford, so that he could be there at the end of the night to walk Zo back to his room.

They made their way down the stairs in silence and then stood outside the doors to their rooms, wrapped in each other's arms, Zo resting his head on Hylas's shoulder.

"Will you come in for a bit?" Zo asked finally.

"I was just about to ask if I might."

"Any time you like."

"Don't say that. It must also be any time *you* like."

Zo nuzzled against him and dropped a kiss lightly on Hylas's jaw. "It is, though. That's what I meant."

Hylas followed him inside, lit the lamp, and steered Zo gently toward the bed.

"I'm afraid, my love, I'm not in any state for—" Zo began, a graceful but clearly automatic speech.

"Don't be ridiculous," Hylas cut him off sternly. "I will sit on the floor and not bother you."

Zo was sitting on the edge of the bed, and Hylas dropped down resolutely to sit at his feet. Zo looked at him for a moment in the semi-darkness, then reached out and took Hylas's face between his hands and rested his cheek against Hylas's hair.

"One might say we should take any opportunity when we're alone together, while we can." He released Hylas and sat back up. "Because when I get a patron, we won't be able to any more."

Hylas nodded. They hadn't spoken of this before, but of course he had understood it. Patronage implied exclusivity; that was the whole point.

"I know. I wish I could offer to be your patron, but … "

There was a moment of charged silence. He realized he'd never said that before.

"Do you?" said Zo finally.

"Yes, of course. I don't mean—I mean because it would help you, because you need a patron. Not because I want any kind of power over you. I want you to be able to rely on me as a friend, not as a … a keeper. Above all I don't want you to be at the mercy of anyone who would treat you unkindly."

Zo nodded, his expression inward. "I wish you could be my patron too, Hylas. I didn't know if you would want it. But I think it would be different, if it were you. The meaning would be different. It's not possible?" He looked up, meeting Hylas's gaze again.

"I don't have the means to support you. I wish I did, I wish more than anything I did."

"Ah. I'm not much accustomed to thinking about money."

Hylas laughed bitterly. "Neither am I, in truth."

Zo made the little noise that Hylas had come to recognize as signalling interest, the way he did when Hylas began to talk about hydraulic engineering or affairs at the government office and stopped because he was afraid of being boring.

"In Ariata, the noble families are forbidden to trade, so they don't use money at all. My mother never liked me to have coins in the house. I used to have my pay directed to an agent who would settle up our accounts with the merchants every month. And when I came to leave Ariata, there was nothing left, I had no savings."

"He'd cheated you."

"Probably, but the truth is I don't know. I hadn't paid enough attention, all those years. I hadn't thought about what my work was worth. I'd felt ashamed to receive pay and glad to get rid of it without having to touch it myself. Now —well, now I couldn't think more differently. I detest this uncertain situation with Loukianos. I want to do my job and be paid for it. Though even if I did, I wouldn't be a fit patron for you. You need—you deserve—a wealthy man."

There was another space of silence. Zo moved to lie down on his bed. He was wearing the earrings that Hylas had given him, and one of them had gotten tangled in his hair. He reached up to loosen it and take it out. Hylas held out a hand to take it for him, and Zo's fingers brushed over his as he dropped the earring into his palm. Zo fiddled for a moment with the other earring.

"I know that it isn't possible," he said, his voice low, "but can you tell me again that you want it?"

"Zo … " Hylas's heart felt over-full. "I want to be yours forever. Your lover, your support, your devoted servant. I can't believe how privileged I am that you want to hear me say that."

Zo pulled out the other earring and half sat up, making a move as if to throw it. He stopped short, the earring clutched in his fist.

"You can't—Hylas, you can't stay here." He looked at Hylas with anger in his eyes. "I'm going to have to take a patron, and if you stay here, next door to me, sharing my garden and coming over to check on me and bring me tea— you can't keep doing that. I'll carry on sleeping with you. I want you so much. Do you think I won't cheat on my patron with you? Hah. I'm a Zashian courtier. Of course I'll do it."

Hylas got to his feet and held out his hand for the other earring. "You will not give your word to be faithful to one man and then betray him. You left the Zashian court because you didn't want to be that kind of man. But if you want me to go, of course I'll go. If my staying would make things hard for you, I won't stay."

Zo handed over the other earring and lay back down.

"I don't want you to go. I'm sorry, I'm—I'm being dramatic. It's not helping."

"You're saying what's in your heart," said Hylas, putting the earrings aside on Zo's dressing table. "I just don't want you to be unhappy. I want you to be with a man who's good for you. I think you can find that."

He came back and resumed his seat on the floor by Zo's bed. He stroked Zo's hair where it lay on the pillow.

"I have until the end of the month," Zo said.

"Why then?"

"Mistress Aula has said I have to secure the patronage of either Timon or Loukianos by Orante's Month."

So she had given him an ultimatum. No wonder he was upset.

"Or what?"

"Or she'll tell everyone who I am. And I—I'm afraid of that."

"Did you tell her why?"

"In general terms—she knows well enough. We had an argument. I couldn't keep my temper."

Hylas sighed. "You shouldn't have to. She says things to you that are hard to forgive. But when it comes to Loukianos … he may be leaving the island before long."

"What?"

He explained what he had learned that day and how the governor seemed resigned to being recalled to Pheme.

"I see," said Zo quietly. "So even if I don't take a patron, you may not be on Tykanos much longer."

"Zo, if that were the case, I would have said so. No, I'll be here. I may just need to find some other way to make a living."

After Hylas left, Zo couldn't sleep. He thought about the way Hylas had said, "If my staying would make things hard for you … " Wouldn't it be hard for *him*, too?

Of course it would. Now that Hylas was letting himself show it, when they were alone together, it was obvious how much he was in love with Zo, and how much it meant to him to be able to give his love physical expression. It would be hard for him to give that up.

But his whole life had been hard. He was resigned to this, the way he'd be resigned to anything. He didn't believe he deserved to be happy, or to continue to be happy. Maybe he thought all he deserved was to have the memory of this short period of happiness to cherish.

What would he say if Zo suggested they leave the Red Balconies together? Of course he'd say yes. Even if it was a terrible idea, burdening himself with an invalid accustomed to luxury, barely able to travel, the two of them with no home, no money, no resources.

He wouldn't say yes because he actually wanted to take Zo away from the Red Balconies, to keep Zo for himself or prevent him from entertaining guests. Of that Zo was sure.

He ran over that morning's conversation with Mistress Aula in his mind, and reluctantly considered the possibility that he could have handled that better. *He* was the one who'd suggested that she wanted to tell all the guests who he was; she'd started simply by saying she wanted to use his identity to the advantage of the house. And he thought of how well Menthe and Pani had managed by giving her a gift, being nicer to her than she had any right to expect.

Hylas had said, "She says things that are hard to forgive." He hadn't said Zo *shouldn't* forgive her.

CHAPTER 19

Zo was asleep in the morning when Hylas came to his door with the tea tray and peeked inside. He set down the tray and retreated quietly, feeling cheated not so much because he'd hoped for another morning of love-making—he'd been preparing to insist, for Zo's sake, that they take it easy that morning anyway—but because he'd wanted to tell Zo what he was planning to do that day. He hoped Zo would approve.

He didn't know that it would work. If Loukianos really was set on resigning and going back to Pheme, asking him for a salary wasn't going to be much use. So the first thing he needed to do was to determine whether Loukianos was serious.

That question was quickly answered once he reached the governor's mansion. There were several sea chests in the atrium of the house. Loukianos had already begun packing up his belongings.

"So have you sent your resignation to Pheme already?" Hylas asked, looking at the chests.

"What?" said Loukianos, rubbing his temple. He showed all the signs of a man who'd been out late the night before drinking. "No, not yet. Just preparing. I really am awfully sorry about this, my dear fellow. The way I told you about everything yesterday was … not decent. I wish you'd come out with us last night, I'd have got to talk to you more."

"I'm here now to talk to you," Hylas pointed out.

"You are, you are. It's very good of you. Let's sit down, shall we?"

He led the way into the official reception room of the mansion, the first time Hylas had ever been shown in there, as far as he could remember.

"Loukianos," he said when they were seated, "we're friends, and I want to be frank with you. I was surprised to learn you're planning to go back to Pheme, because you have not been acting like someone whose career is on the line. You gave me no indication, before yesterday, that the aqueduct was urgent for you—I knew it was urgent for the town, but that's a different thing. You've been—I've been strategizing with Mutari while you've been … what? What have you been doing?"

Loukianos waved a hand with a sad look. "She'd make a better governor than I do."

That was very much not the point. "She's doing a lot of work that you ought to be doing, is what I'm trying to say. And she doesn't *get* to be governor, no matter how good she'd be at it. She doesn't get to live in your mansion, she doesn't get paid by the Phemian government. She's using what power she has to help Tykanos because it's her home—you have a lot more power and you should be doing the same thing."

For a moment, Loukianos looked ready to become offended. Then he sagged back into his chair. "You're right, I … No, you're right."

Hylas pressed on: "The aqueduct absolutely is necessary, and Mutari and I have made progress—we still need permission from Tetum, but the other obstacles have been dealt with, and I have a workable design well underway. But there's more to be done with the town's water supply than just the

198

aqueduct, and I have been doing some of it. If you'd write to Pheme and tell them the work that's been done so far, instead of preparing your resignation … "

Loukianos gave him a startled look. "But I didn't do any of that. I don't even know what you're talking about."

"I've mapped the island's water system," said Hylas patiently. "Yes, there was a map in the government office, it's very nice, but it was also very out of date. I've been having repairs made all over the town. I've pinpointed the problem at the new bath complex and think I know how to solve it. I haven't done anything at the fort yet, but only because … "

He paused as he realized how that sentence should finish. *Only because I've been afraid to go to the fort to talk to them about it.* He'd been avoiding contact with the fort as much as he could, ever since coming to the island—he hadn't even gone down to the fort when he needed men to help dig up the roads—without even thinking about why. But he knew why; it was because it reminded him too much of home.

That was no reason at all. The officers at the fort weren't going to look at him and see a failed man, a proscribed aristocrat, the way the Ariatan noblemen had. They would look at him and see an engineer. And they needed an engineer.

"The point is," he said, picking up the thread of the conversation as if he hadn't just had an epiphany, "I don't know what you think I've been doing all this time, but it hasn't been nothing. I've made real improvements in the town, I have more planned, and you should tell Pheme that."

"I should take credit for your work, you mean?"

"Absolutely. It's what you intended to do when you brought me here to build the aqueduct."

"Well, I—I mean … " Loukianos looked flustered.

"You more or less told me so yesterday," Hylas reminded him. "And I already knew it, anyway. It's why you haven't been paying me a salary."

"I just thought … it would be simpler … You haven't been lacking for money, have you?"

"This isn't recrimination, Loukianos. I understand what you were doing. I didn't question it when you first hired me, but my situation has changed, and I need a salary now."

"I'll see what I can—I don't know if—"

"No, I wasn't asking you for it." He said it as if that wasn't precisely what he had come up here to do; but he'd thought of a better option. "I'm going down to the fort this afternoon to ask for a permanent post."

"Oh, but they don't just … I mean, you can't … "

"Maybe I can't. Maybe I'll need to write a letter in verse to somebody's mistress and go round all the tea houses dropping hints and hire a soothsayer to find somebody's illegitimate son—but actually I'm going to just walk in the door with a lot of maps and plans and make my case. I think it's worth a try. I want to stay on the island. I'm going to put a little effort into it."

Loukianos nodded. "Right." After a long silence, he said, "And what you're saying is, you think I should do the same."

"I do. If you want to stay. If you want to resign and leave Tykanos—"

"Gods, I don't. I truly don't. You know—" He leaned forward in his chair. "I've been thinking of something. Prince Zoharaza."

"Oh?" said Hylas warily. "What about him?"

"Well, you know he was a hostage at King Nahazra's court. And I was wondering—would they want him back? Yes, you know—" He popped up from his seat and began pacing. "What if I sent him back? What if I turned him over to the Zashian crown? It might be a useful move. I doubt they'd be so ready to recall me to Pheme if I'd done a favour for the king of Zash." He whirled around to look excitedly at Hylas. "It's just the kind of thing I should be doing, isn't it?"

"What? No! It's the opposite of what you should be

doing." Hylas stood up to face him. "Intriguing and back-stabbing and acting like a … like a despot? No. You're going to do favours for the king of Zash? You think he was right to hold the son of one of his vassals hostage, so you're going to *give him back*? Loukianos. You're a government official from a republic. You uphold the laws of Pheme—you don't trade prisoners with a foreign king in hopes of some convoluted favour. Also … " He paused for breath. "Zo and I are lovers. *Do not* threaten him."

Loukianos's eyes had grown very wide. He took a step back from Hylas. "You. And Prince Zoharaza. Are?"

"A couple," said Hylas evenly. Distantly he registered that he wasn't even blushing. "Yes."

"Hylas, I had no idea! I didn't even know that you … " Loukianos gestured vaguely. "But Zoharaza? Immortal gods. I remember him from when he was just a boy, and they were already writing poems about him at the court. Pretty sedate poems—I mean, it was Sasia—but he definitely had admir-ers. And you and … Immortal gods. Congratulations! You must want to get him out of the Red Balconies."

"Loukianos … " If there was a stick in sight, the man could be trusted to get the wrong end of it. "I *want* to keep him safe. I want for you not to use him as a bargaining token with the Sasian crown."

"No, no, no—my dear friend, I will never do that. I swear to you on my life."

Hylas nodded and felt some of the tension relax in his jaw and his shoulders. He couldn't remember the last time he had been so angry, and yet so confident that he could master the situation. Maybe when he had stood up to the chief engi-neer about that shitty cement in the dam above Koilas. This had felt a little bit like that.

After this, he was not going to have any problem with the naval officers.

"It would be better if you didn't use the name Prince

Zoharaza too much in conversation," he added. "If you didn't talk too much about who he used to be. He goes by Zo, and he's a companion at the Red Balconies. His health is fragile, and it's a safe and comfortable place for him. I would not want him to have to leave."

Loukianos was still staring as if his eyes might fall out of his head, but he nodded.

Zo ate breakfast alone, furious with himself for oversleeping and missing one of his precious mornings with Hylas. His mood wasn't improved when Chrestos came tapping on his door with a guilty expression.

"Please don't hate me."

Zo groaned. "What did you say, and who did you say it to?"

"It wasn't me, it was Themi—I mean, I mean the only person I told was Captain Themistokles, and I forgot to mention it was a secret, because I thought he'd know, but he didn't realize and said something to Taris, thinking she already knew, and she told, well … "

"Well?"

"Well, everybody. I'm *sorry*. Please don't hate me."

"Mistress Aula knows?"

"No! No, everyone knows better than to tell her. I think everyone knows better than to tell her. But—but we're all really happy about it, Zo. We all love the aqueduct man and think you two are perfect for each other."

Zo was surprised to find it made him happy to hear that. He tried not to show it, because Chrestos had really been an ass, telling his patron and not mentioning that it was a secret. Hylas was going to find Captain Themistokles apologizing to him before the end of the day, Zo was sure, and would be confused and embarrassed by it.

"I'm glad you all approve," Zo said. "Just *please* don't let Mistress know—she's already annoyed enough with me."

"She might allow it, though, like she did with Pani and Menthe," Chrestos suggested hopefully.

"But did she find out about Pani and Menthe because everybody was gossiping about them and she was the last to know?"

"Er, no—she found out because they told her, I think, after they surprised her with the frescoes. Oh! I get it. You want to tell her yourself, at the right moment."

"Something like that," said Zo.

He went up to Mistress Aula's room after Chrestos left. She looked surprised to see him when she opened her door. She had a bowl of tea in her hand.

"Do you need something?" she asked.

"I wanted to talk to you."

"Well, come in." She held the door open.

He came inside, and they sat on the divan. The doors were open onto her balcony on the front of the house.

"That smells good," he said, indicating the tea. "Is it a new blend?"

"Yes, just something I'm trying out. Chamomile flowers, lavender buds, and a hint of cinnamon." She hesitated. "Here, have a taste and tell me what you think. I don't have another bowl." She passed him the one she was holding.

He took it and sipped. "Mmm. It's nice. Subtle."

"It's quite wholesome and doesn't keep you awake. I thought we could serve it in the evenings." She took the bowl back from him. "Well, what is it?"

"I'm sorry that I lost my temper with you yesterday."

"No, you're not," she said sourly. "You think I'm a harpy for not believing you're really ill. Theano's already come and set me straight about it, all right? I understand. I'm in the wrong. Just because you're not sick all the time doesn't mean it's an act."

Zo decided not to respond to that. He repeated himself calmly: "I'm sorry for losing my temper because I realize now that you weren't actually threatening me. You were just asking how we could make something of my being a prince. For the good of the house."

She looked at him and drew a breath as if about to speak, then closed her mouth. After a moment she opened it again: "I ... I suppose I *was* thinking of telling everyone who you are, and I suppose if you have enemies ... that might not be safe."

He made a rueful face. "That's the problem."

After a moment she said, "I understand why that made you angry. You don't need to apologize."

"I do want to help the house, though. Like the others. We all want the Red Balconies to thrive. I was thinking, if you wanted to throw out hints ... "

"How do you mean?"

"Oh, you know. Tell one man one thing, another something else—make it all sound like secrets they must swear to keep ... I don't mind cultivating a bit of mystique."

She looked thoughtful. "That could work. It might even be better than trying to tell everyone your whole story. It is a little far-fetched, after all."

"Exactly. Sometimes I'm not sure I believe it myself."

She laughed shortly. "That's very fair of you. I realize I haven't always been fair."

"Neither have I."

"I suppose you have your pride to consider. Being—well, a prince, and all that. On the subject of a patron ... "

"I am working on that," he said automatically. "But ... "

"Have you considered the aqueduct man?" she said before he could finish his thought.

"Have I ... what?"

She went on quickly, as if this was something she'd given thought to: "I know the two of you are friends. And he certainly seems to pay attention to you in the evenings—if he'd been any other guest, I'd have said he was smitten, but he's awfully hard to read. Though you'll know better than I do.

"I just thought, if we could get him—you know, he's got quite a name on the island already. Everybody knows him, he's a friend of the governor's, chaperoned Mutari from the Peacock on a trip to Tetum, which means he's one of your sort, or the quartermaster would never have allowed that. It's good to have him as a tenant, but having him as a patron would be better."

"Interesting," said Zo. "Do you think so?"

"Well … I know he's not wealthy, but there are other things to consider. And to be honest, I like him better than Timon of Kos *or* Governor Loukianos."

"I'll see what I can do," said Zo.

"I'm glad the two of you found each other," said Menthe privately to Zo as they were setting up for the evening's guests. "I take back what I said about it being a bad idea to take up with someone living in the house. So long as you don't rush into these things … "

Zo laughed. "With Hylas? No fear of that."

The mood that night was as warm as the evening air. The guests remarked on it when they began arriving.

"How could we not be happy?" said Theano. "The weather is fine, the days are growing longer, and there is still light in the sky."

They were sitting out in the courtyard, the first time since the fall. Hylas had not come home yet, and a couple of Zo's regular guests had talked him into taking up his flute. He heard some shuffling around of the people on his left, and someone slipped in to sit beside him.

"I'd rather you put that pretty mouth to a different use, Your Highness," said a familiar voice, pitched low, but not really low enough.

Zo was proud of himself for not missing a note and finishing out the piece without glancing over at Timon. He finished playing and laid the flute in his lap to take a drink of wine.

"I heard an interesting tale about you at the Sunset Palace," said Timon.

Zo smiled blandly at him. "Oh yes?"

"Is it true you used to be a prince?"

"I didn't stop being one. It isn't an elected office."

"Hm. Not much of a prince, though, are you? Not a *real* prince."

"Oh, absolutely not, no. May I pour you some wine?" He picked up the wine pot, holding his sleeve delicately. "My homeland has been a vassal state of Zash for a century. We are proud of our lineage, but we have no real power."

Timon slurped his wine. He had an unnecessarily noisy way of drinking that irritated Zo. It was one of those things that would have been innocuous, could even have become endearing, if the man himself had been likeable. Instead it seemed almost sinister.

"What would your father the king think if he knew his royal son was whoring out his sweet ass to foreign cocks?"

Zo stared at him, for a moment too startled to respond. He could not—must not—look around to see who else in the courtyard had heard that. Timon had spoken at a normal volume, and there were other guests nearby.

"Timon," he said finally, "you and I have shared hours of pleasant conversation. I have entertained you, offered you attention, intimacy. We parted amicably. Why would you go out of your way to say something so hurtful to me?"

For a moment, gratifyingly, Timon was too wrong-footed

to respond. Apparently sincerity was the last thing he had expected from Zo.

"You think we 'parted amicably'?" Timon said petulantly. "You threw me over, you—you spat in my face as if you think you're not just a whore. This isn't Sasia, Your Highness."

"You needn't use any title, but the correct one, actually—"

"I don't give a shit!" He was still enough in control that he had not raised his voice to a disruptive volume, and though other people around them might be hearing this, no one felt it necessary to intervene. "You tried to throw me over, and you don't get to do that. This isn't Sasia. You're not a prince here. Your tea house is falling down around your ears, and you think you can still *choose* who you say yes or no to?"

Zo was rattled, and he hated himself for it. He had felt safe for so long in his refuge at the Red Balconies that he had forgotten what it was like to be threatened, and this was a new kind of threat, overt and ugly.

"If you imagine I am friendless and desperate, you are very much mistaken." That was true, so why did the words sound hollow to Zo when he said them?

Cheerful raised voices from the other side of the courtyard drew Zo's attention, and he looked up to see that Hylas had just returned. The lamplight glowed in his hair, and surely he looked taller and more handsome than the last time Zo had seen him? Maybe it was just the way that he was smiling, so much at ease and at home in the Red Balconies courtyard. He waved at Zo.

And then he headed for the passage to their rooms. He was not staying.

"If I tell your mistress I'm ready to become your patron," Timon said, "there'll be nothing you can do about it. You'll be mine, Your Highness."

"That is not how it works," Zo said between clenched teeth.

He wished he could feel more sure that was true.

Of course Hylas couldn't stay and burn incense every night. He was making an effort to save money; he'd told Zo as much. But he had looked so happy, Zo had just assumed he was going to come and sit down with the other guests.

Mercifully, at this point a new arrival saw Zo's flute and begged in flowery terms for some music, which gave Zo an excuse to ignore Timon for a while. Timon sat there slurping his wine; Zo could feel the man's gaze on the side of his face. He launched into the longest piece he knew.

He stopped playing finally, exhausted, and registered that a hush had fallen over the guests. He didn't think it was related to his music. He looked up. Everyone seemed to be looking in the same direction, and he realized Hylas was back in the courtyard.

Hylas was standing just outside the circle of guests gathered around Zo, and in his hands he held a ring of rosemary branches woven into a garland.

Zo dropped his flute with a gasp.

"Eh?" said Timon, the last to catch on. "What—"

Someone moved aside to let Hylas come into the circle. He looked a fraction less at ease than he had when Zo had glimpsed him returning to the house, but still, if you knew him, you could tell he was brimming with resolve, full of joy to be doing this.

"Zo," he said, "I would like to offer you this." He held out the garland.

There was no way Zo could have got to his feet, but he didn't need to because Hylas knelt in front of him. Zo took the garland and settled it on his head. There were gasps and cries of excitement from all around the courtyard. The scent of the rosemary was intoxicating.

Timon had started to shout something in protest—"How

dare you?" and something about "a stuttering, red-haired bricklayer"—but the other guests shushed him. One of Zo's regulars began loudly reciting a famous poem about a mortal in love with a nymph who gets chosen as the consort of a god, a traditional piece for such situations, and someone else began loudly ribbing him for being unoriginal.

Hylas and Zo just sat at the centre of it all, smiling at one another.

Mistress Aula and Taris were clasping hands and bouncing up and down excitedly like little girls. Zo thought he heard Chrestos telling people that he'd "known it all along," whatever that meant. Ahmos came and discreetly escorted Timon out.

Hylas reached for Zo's hand and clasped it. "We could retire to your room," he said. "Couldn't we?"

"I guess we could. Let's."

Hylas picked up Zo's flute and helped him to his feet. Zo took his arm and leaned on it, doing his best to make it look elegant for their audience, but also really needing the support. Hylas, to Zo's surprise, turned to wave to the crowd before they left.

"That was *perfect*," Zo murmured as they exited the courtyard. "How are you so wonderful? My face hurts from smiling so much. I don't care if it's not real—"

"It is real," said Hylas seriously. He stopped in the dark anteroom, turning to face Zo, both his hands warm on Zo's arms, steadying him. "I went down to the fort and presented a case for the navy appointing me chief engineer for the island. They agreed on the spot. I didn't expect that—I guess I was persuasive. I certainly felt as if I could have talked anyone into anything, if it was for your sake. It won't make me rich, but I don't think you need me to be rich. You'd only need a rich man if he was supporting a wife and a household as well as you. I don't need to do that. You … you are my household, Zo. If you—as long as you—want to be."

209

Zo wrapped his arms around Hylas and hugged him fiercely. He felt tears gathering in his eyes.

"Hylas, if you want … I'll leave the Red Balconies with you."

"All right," said Hylas easily, stroking Zo's back. "Where should we go? To the market? The beach?"

"No, I mean … " He wiped his eyes and looked up at Hylas, though he couldn't really see him in the dark. "I mean to live with you somewhere other than here."

"Oh. You'd do that, if I wanted?"

"I would. Gladly."

Zo felt Hylas draw a deep breath and let it out. "I thought you might. But do you want to?"

Zo hesitated.

"Because I don't want you to," Hylas said. "Not as long as you're happy here. If that should change … if you *want* to leave, we'll leave in an instant, together."

"You want to stay here. At the Red Balconies."

Hylas drew him closer. "I like it here. It's a good place for you. You get to see people without going out, to put your skills to use. You have your garden. Our garden. You have me next door. I do want to stay here, yes. On Tykanos, in this house. With you."

Zo rested his head on Hylas's shoulder, and the rosemary garland gave off a renewed burst of scent as the leaves were bruised.

"Let's go in to bed," he murmured.

"Yes, my prince," said Hylas.

EPILOGUE

THEY WENT to the beach a couple of days later. They had intended to go by themselves, but Chrestos overheard Hylas asking Mistress Aula about hiring a chair for Zo, and somehow he got the idea that it was a general outing and began inviting other people. So when they were ready to set off, they found Chrestos and Captain Themistokles waiting by the front door with a picnic basket, trying to talk Theano into bringing Leta, who had never been to the seashore.

"Is this everyone, then?" Chrestos said brightly. "Then let's be off!"

They set off down the streets of the town toward the seashore, everyone taking turns carrying the baby, while the bearers that Hylas had hired carried Zo in a light sedan chair.

"I heard he's a prince," Themistokles remarked. "Was he taken prisoner or something? Did he have amnesia?"

"No, no," said Hylas absently. He had been contemplating a design for a sedan chair with wheels so that one person could pull it, or maybe push it. "He's the youngest son of some warlord from a corner of Sasia that nobody's ever heard of. He's *something* like a prince, but he never advertised the fact."

"Mm," said Themistokles approvingly. "Probably thought it would sound tacky. Good fellow."

They arrived at the beach and spread out their blankets and set their picnic things in the sand. Theano took Leta to wade in the surf, and Chrestos and Captain Themistokles went for a stroll together. Zo lay down and put his head in Hylas's lap.

"How do you feel?" Hylas asked, stroking Zo's hair.

Zo tipped his head back and smiled up at him. "Good. Not tired at all."

"I'm sorry we're not alone."

Zo laughed. "That's all right. We can be alone in our garden any time."

The beach was not as deserted as it had been when Hylas visited it before with Loukianos. He spotted another couple strolling in the distance toward where Chrestos and Themistokles were headed, and a party seated in the sand with baskets and blankets at the opposite end of the beach.

"Should we get up and wade in the water?" Zo said presently.

Hylas helped Zo to his feet, and Zo leaned on his arm as they walked down to the water. Leta was now back on the dry sand, picking up seashells. Zo rolled up his trousers and walked into the shallow water. The sea breeze blew his hair back from his face, and he closed his eyes, smiling.

"Hello, Hylas! Hello, Theano!"

Hylas turned with surprise to see Mutari coming down the beach toward them, followed by two men. One of them was the quartermaster, the other Nahaz, the Sasian regular from the Red Balconies.

They all greeted one another, and Mutari made introductions which turned out to be largely unnecessary, because Nahaz already knew everyone from the Red Balconies.

"Oh, I didn't know you frequented the house," said

Mutari. "It is the oldest on the island, you know, carrying on a proud tradition."

"Ah, indeed?" said Nahaz. "It is a most charming place. I have been there many times. I feel ... almost as if it is a second home. They took me in and cared for me one night when I was injured in the street."

"Truly?" said Mutari, wide-eyed. "Blessed Orante! You must tell us the story of that some time."

Chrestos and Themistokles came back along the beach at this point, bringing with them the other couple who had been walking on the sand.

"Hylas! Hello!"

It was Governor Loukianos, with the companion from the Bower of Suos who had thought Hylas and Loukianos were a couple. The companion looked more resigned than pleased to be joining the growing crowd of people at the water's edge.

There was another desultory round of introductions; most of them knew one another. The governor remembered to introduce Zo as "Zo."

"Theano," said Loukianos, looking at her with a strange, subdued expression. "How, er, how have you been?"

"I have been well, sir."

Leta toddled up brandishing a seashell she had found. "Shell, Mama, shell!"

Mutari's party was starting to wander away down the beach with Chrestos and Captain Themistokles. The companion from the Bower was looking at the sand as if considering hunting for seashells himself.

"She's your daughter," said Loukianos, staring fixedly at Leta.

"Her name is Leta." Theano bent and picked up the child. "Say hello, Leta." Leta buried her face in her mother's neck and peeked out shyly.

Hylas took Zo's hand and drew him away from the shore. They waded out until the water was lapping the hem of Hylas's tunic and Zo's trousers were soaked, then they reached a sandbar where it grew shallower again.

"Leta's father," said Hylas, "Theano's former patron—he died before she was born, didn't he? What was his name?"

"Hippolytos."

"I thought so. He was Governor Loukianos's lover. I don't think Loukianos knew there was a child."

They stood on the sandbar, looking back at the group on the shore. Loukianos was holding Leta now.

"Hm," said Zo. "It seems it wasn't me you needed to introduce him to at the Red Balconies after all."

Hylas put his arm around Zo's waist, and Zo leaned against him.

"Shall we go back to shore?" Hylas asked.

"Look, Mutari's waving to you." Zo pointed.

Mutari had left the men of her party and was gesturing to Hylas and Zo from the edge of the water. They waded back down off the sandbar into the deeper water toward her, and she picked up her skirt and came through the surf to meet them.

"Hylas! I had to seize the moment to tell you. Nahaz, over there? He's the Gylphian envoy to Tykanos."

"No!"

"Yes! He's been 'incognito' because his post wasn't set to start until next month. And you've been wooing him at the Red Balconies this whole time. We're getting our aqueduct, Hylas."

"We're getting our aqueduct." In the most Tykanos way possible, it seemed, but that, Hylas realized, he could live with.

"Hooray!" Zo gave an elegant and discreet little cheer. Hylas tightened the arm that he still had around his waist.

"And *you* have a boyfriend," said Mutari accusingly. "Why on earth did you tell me that you didn't?"

She turned and splashed back to the dry sand, laughing, before he could muster an explanation.

JOIN THE CLUB

Join my *Fragments Club* list to get exclusive short stories and snippets!

Sign up at **sextonscottage.com**

ACKNOWLEDGMENTS

As always, I am deeply grateful to Alexandra Bolintineanu for her wise suggestions and moral support, and to May Peterson for her inspired editing. Mary Beth Decker generously helped me polish the cover copy. Flora Kirk was a joy to work with as she created the cover image, which captures the setting and the main characters perfectly.

I especially want to thank KJ Charles, who has been an inspiration and helped me in very practical ways ever since I started writing romance. To have one of my favourite authors be excited about reading my books—it really doesn't get better than that.

Although my setting is a historical patchwork, I do a lot of research on real places and times. Two books I found especially useful when writing *The House of the Red Balconies* are Georgia L. Irby's *Using and Conquering the Watery World in Greco-Roman Antiquity* and Alexandra Croom's *Running the Roman Home*. The latter in particular is a book I wish I'd discovered years earlier, though I won't mention what details I might have changed in my previous books as a result.

Finally, as a researcher without a university affiliation, I'm grateful to have discovered Perlego, a digital academic library that gives me access to titles I couldn't get otherwise, and also allows me to relive that "browsing the stacks for random stuff" feeling from my university days.

In a walled fortress with no way in or out lives the beaten hero of the Western Mountains, imprisoned by his enemies. Up the mountain one spring comes a young man to be his bride—and to kill him. But nothing goes according to plan.

Lion & Snake is an mm romance set in a fictional world inspired by the Ancient Near East.

Find out more: reamstories.com/ajdemas

ALSO BY A.J. DEMAS

AS ALICE DEGAN

ABOUT THE AUTHOR

A.J. Demas is an ex-academic who formerly studied and taught medieval literature, and now writes romance set in a fictional world based on an entirely different era. She lives in Ontario, Canada, with her husband and cute daughter.

Find out about upcoming books and more here:
www.ajdemas.com

A.J. also publishes fantasy and historical fiction with a metaphysical twist under a different name (her real one). You can find those here: www.alicedegan.com

Made in the USA
Middletown, DE
11 July 2024